AMERICAN ★ HISTORY

U.S. POLITICAL PARTIES
Development and Division

By Philip Wolny

LUCENT
P R E S S

Published in 2019 by
Lucent Press, an Imprint of Greenhaven Publishing, LLC
353 3rd Avenue
Suite 255
New York, NY 10010

Designer: Deanna Paternostro
Editor: Jessica Moore

Library of Congress Cataloging-in-Publication Data

Names: Wolny, Philip, author.
Title: U.S. political parties : development and division / Philip Wolny.
Description: New York : Lucent Press, 2019. | Series: American history |
  Includes bibliographical references and index.
Identifiers: LCCN 2018010740| ISBN 9781534564244 (library bound book) | ISBN
  9781534564268 (pbk. book) | ISBN 9781534564251 (e-book)
Subjects: LCSH: Political parties--United States--History.
Classification: LCC JK2261 .W676 2019 | DDC 324.273--dc23
LC record available at https://lccn.loc.gov/2018010740

Printed in the United States of America

CPSIA compliance information: Batch #BS18KL: For further information contact Greenhaven Publishing LLC, New York, New York
at 1-844-317-7404.

Please visit our website, www.greenhavenpublishing.com. For a free color catalog of all our high-quality books, call toll free 1-844-317-7404 or fax 1-844-317-7405.

Contents

Foreword · 4

Setting the Scene: A Timeline · 6

Introduction:
Understanding Political Parties · 8

Chapter One:
The Dawn of American Politics · 11

Chapter Two:
Democrats and Whigs · 23

Chapter Three:
Republicans and Democrats · 35

Chapter Four:
The New Century · 49

Chapter Five:
The New Deal Era · 62

Chapter Six:
Political Parties Then and Now · 74

Epilogue:
The Journey Ahead · 88

Notes · 95

For More Information · 97

Index · 99

Picture Credits · 103

About the Author · 104

Foreword

The United States is a relatively young country. It has existed as its own nation for more than 200 years, but compared to nations such as China that have existed since ancient times, it is still in its infancy. However, the United States has grown and accomplished much since its birth in 1776. What started as a loose confederation of former British colonies has grown into a major world power whose influence is felt around the globe.

How did the United States manage to develop into a global superpower in such a short time? The answer lies in a close study of its unique history. The story of America is unlike any other—filled with colorful characters, a variety of exciting settings, and events too incredible to be anything other than true.

Too often, the experience of history is lost among the basic facts: names, dates, places, laws, treaties, and battles. These fill countless textbooks, but they are rarely compelling on their own. Far more interesting are the stories that surround those

basic facts. It is in discovering those stories that students are able to see history as a subject filled with life—and a subject that says as much about the present as it does about the past.

The titles in this series allow readers to immerse themselves in the action at pivotal historical moments. They also encourage readers to discuss complex issues in American history—many of which still affect Americans today. These include racism, states' rights, civil liberties, and many other topics that are in the news today but have their roots in the earliest days of America. As such, readers are encouraged to think critically about history and current events.

Each title is filled with excellent tools for research and analysis. Fully cited quotations from historical figures, letters, speeches, and documents provide students with firsthand accounts of major events. Primary sources bring authority to the text, as well. Sidebars highlight these quotes and primary sources, as well as interesting figures and events. Annotated bibliographies allow students to locate and evaluate sources for further information on the subject.

A deep understanding of America's past is necessary to understand its present and its future. Sometimes you have to look back in order to see how to best move forward, and that is certainly true when writing the next chapter in the American story.

1788
The new government of the United States is formed via the ratification of the U.S. Constitution, set up as a balance of powers among legislative, judicial, and executive branches.

1828
The election of Andrew Jackson over John Quincy Adams begins the era of Jacksonian democracy, a new chapter in partisan politics.

1800
Thomas Jefferson's victory over John Adams ends the reign of the Federalist Party and begins that of the Democratic-Republicans.

1833
The Whig Party is formed to oppose Andrew Jackson and the Democrats.

1788	1788–1789	1796	1800	1828	1833	1854	1860

1854
The Republican Party is formed, largely in opposition to slavery, replacing the fading Whigs as the main opposition party to the Democrats.

1788–1789
The first U.S. presidential election is conducted with the unopposed, nonpartisan election of George Washington.

1860
Abraham Lincoln is elected president, triggering the secession of the Southern slave states and igniting the American Civil War, which lasted from 1861 to 1865.

1796
Federalist John Adams and Democratic-Republican Thomas Jefferson face off in America's first election where political parties—the Federalists and the Democratic-Republicans—played a role.

A Timeline

1896
William McKinley, the Republican presidential candidate, beats William Jennings Bryan, the Democratic candidate, in a contest that set a Progressive agenda for the following elections.

1932
In response to the Great Depression, Americans vote the Republicans out of office and elect Democrat Franklin D. Roosevelt, whose New Deal programs would realign politics for the next few decades.

2000
The presidential election is bitterly contested in Florida, leading to a Supreme Court battle that declares Florida's vote count for Republican candidate George W. Bush against Al Gore.

| 1896 | 1932 | 1968 | 1980 | 1992 | 2000 | 2008 | 2016 |

1968
Republican Richard Nixon uses the "southern strategy" and exploits the Democratic Party's division over the Vietnam War to win the presidency.

1980
Ronald Reagan draws Republicans and some Democrats, winning by a landslide against incumbent Democratic president Jimmy Carter.

1992
In a three-way race against Republican incumbent George H. W. Bush and Independent Ross Perot, Democrat Bill Clinton reclaims the presidency for his party.

2008
Democrat Barack Obama beats his Republican opponent, John McCain, to become the nation's first black president.

2016
The highly partisan and unpredictable presidential election divides America, and a victory by Donald J. Trump over Hillary Clinton sets the stage for further division between the political parties.

UNDERSTANDING POLITICAL PARTIES

It is rare to watch the news or go online today without hearing or reading about Democrats and Republicans and how they compete for power, whether on the local, state, or national levels. A person may even hear mention of smaller "third" parties, such as the Green Party, whose platform promotes environmentalism and social justice, or the Libertarians, who believe in minimal (or no) government interference in personal or economic matters.

Political parties have existed since America's birth. U.S. history has partly been a story of the struggles among two or more parties. Elected leaders at the forefront and party officials behind the scenes have been some of the most important figures in the nation's development.

Members of parties organize themselves according to beliefs and goals. Parties debate where to place government efforts and resources. Some might believe that more money should be put into the military and law enforcement, while others believe in helping those who have low incomes with free health care, education, and even housing. From the Far Left to the center to the Far Right on the political spectrum, people with all types of viewpoints pool their efforts and resources and try to accomplish things that align with their worldviews.

Development and Division

The story of political parties in the United States is one of development and division, of splitting apart to come together again, and of a set of processes repeated over and over. The Republicans at the dawn of the nation's history were different from the Republican Party that rose against slavery in the 1850s and whose beliefs Abraham Lincoln supported. The Democrats of the late 19th century—who

Televised debates are a common element of political campaigns and one of the ways that parties present their ideas and candidates to the public.

supported laws that treated black Americans as second-class citizens—are different from the Democrats of the 1960s, whose efforts went a long way to fix the shameful legacies of segregation and oppression via the efforts of President Lyndon B. Johnson and others. Other parties arose and then quickly collapsed, such as the Federalists and the Whigs.

Political parties themselves are not static, or unchanging, entities. Their membership and opinions may change over time. Often, different groups within a party, or factions, can push or pull a party in one direction or the other. They may take the lead and become pioneers of a whole new attitude or idea. Just as

often, and sometimes more so, party leaders can be slow to adapt to change. They might be a collection of interest groups and factions that agree on some things and disagree on others, working together on some efforts and sitting out others. Conflict within parties can weaken and even crush them, or it may leave them stronger than ever.

Cutthroat Politics

Politics has always been a rough and tumble game, often dirty and cutthroat. The era of broadsheet newspapers with shocking headlines, rigged ballot boxes, and paying for votes is not as far from modern problems of gerrymandering (manipulation of boundaries of

Emotions run high at the conclusion of elections, when supporters, campaign workers, and volunteers discover whether their efforts have led their candidate or cause to victory.

electoral districts to give a certain party an unfair advantage over others), social media fights, and television attack ads as people would like to believe. Some believe that today's political landscape is hopeless and that many politicians are greedy opportunists. Others feel that their politicians, whether in their state's capital or Washington, D.C., are completely removed from the interests of ordinary citizens.

Still, political movements rise and fall, and these movements often respond to the pressing issues of their time. New groups of idealistic and enthusiastic young people take over for the older and experienced ones who step aside. As the history of political parties shows, pressing social issues often cause the views of parties to change, and the Democratic and Republican parties of today may differ drastically from those that will exist in five, ten, or twenty years.

Chapter One

THE DAWN OF AMERICAN POLITICS

Even before the founding of the United States, American elites formed political factions. At the end of the 18th century, when revolutionaries split the 13 American colonies from the rule of Great Britain, there was no instantaneous communication over long distances. Today's modern, hour-long airplane flight took weeks on horseback in the 1700s. The main place to get news and for people to spread their political views was on paper. These included political messages in books and periodicals such as newspapers and posters, called broadsides, that people put in town squares and visible public places.

Ironing Out a Constitution

The participants in the 1787 Constitutional Convention were largely an elite group of wealthy statesmen and businesspeople. Sometimes collectively known as the Framers, others played major roles in the American Revolution. Although the constitution they crafted does not actually mention political parties or factions, their fight to have the individual states ratify the document and the struggles that took place in defining what it contained would carry over into the dawning era of American politics. The earliest political factions that arose around the Constitutional Convention would continue to struggle over the direction of the new government and the country's future well after all 13 of the first U.S. states had ratified it by 1790.

On one side were the Federalists. They favored a strong federal, or national, government, with some authority over the states themselves. Political parties in their later form were unknown during the colonial period. Many believed they were a bad idea, but the Federalists slowly developed into an actual party throughout the 1790s. The leader of the Federalists

THE COLONIAL GAZETTE

Num. 39.]   SUPPLEMENT.   Price 2 Pence

Oct.   1781

LETTER FROM GEN. WASHINGTON TO THE GOVERNOR OF MARYLAND, ANNOUNCING THE SURRENDER OF CORNWALLIS.

CAMP NEAR YORK, OCT., 1781.

DEAR SIR : Inclosed I have the honor of transmitting to your Excellency the terms upon which Lord Cornwallis has surrendered the Garrisons of York and Gloucester.

We have not been able yet to get an account of prisoners, ordnance or stores in the different departments; but from the best general report there will be (officers included) upwards of seven thousand men, besides seamen, more than 70 pieces of brass ordnance and a hundred of iron, their stores and other valuable articles.

My present engagements will not allow me to add more than my congratulations on this happy event, and to express the high sense I have of the powerful aid which i have derived from the State of Maryland in complying with my every request to the execution of it. The prisoners will be divided between Winchester, in Virginia, and Fort Frederick, in Maryland. With every sentiment of the most perfect esteem and regard, I have the honor to be

Your Excellency : most obedient and humble servant,   G. WASHINGTON.

The French at Yorktown.

Few things, indeed, suggested by the history of the war are more instructive than a parallel between the fate of Burgoyne and the fate of Cornwallis. The defeat of Washington on Long Island and the loss of New York had been attributed to the fact that his troops were raw militia. Yet it was mainly with just such men, and not with Continentals (as the regular soldiers of the united colonies were called), that the American commanders in northern New York overcame, in two successive battles, the well-disciplined and admirably appointed army of Burgoyne. This was the one brilliant military triumph achieved by either party in the whole course of the struggle; yet, strange to say, its most substantial fruit was its favorable effect on the negotiations which for two years Franklin had been pushing at the court of Versailles. It was not, however, until the beginning of the ensuing year that the French Ministry would even promise assistance to the colonies; and although their advances of money may from that time forward be said to have kept the continental army on its feet, they did not render effective military aid until the arrival of Count De Grasse in the Chesapeake, about the beginning of September, 1781.

The surrender of Cornwallis was the direct result of the advantage gained by De Grasse over Admiral Graves in the naval battle which took place off the mouth of Chesapeake Bay on September 5, 1781. For the first time during the war, the English failed to have a preponderance of naval strength in American waters, and for almost the first time an English Admiral, commanding a force not greatly inferior to his opponents, sailed postiteinimously away after an indecisive action, in which the French loss in killed and wounded was actually the greater. After this unexpected and inexcusable behaviour on the part of an English naval officer, the surrender of Cornwallis was clearly an obvious necessity. On one side there was the French fleet, comprising twenty four ships of the line

carrying 1,700 guns, and 19,000 seamen. On the land side was Rochambeau with French troops, aggregating 8,400 men, and 5,500 Continental troops under Washington, together with 3,000 militia, who were of less account. Against this military and naval force, Cornwallis had 7,500 men within the works of Yorktown, exclusive of 800 marines, disembarked from some English frigate which had lain in the river. Under these circumstances the surrender of the English force was plainly a mere question of time. It may be said, however, that the presence of the land force at a place where it could so happily co operate with the French fleet, bears witness to great strategical ability, and it has been usual to give the credit of the combination to Washington. It is clear, however, that throughout the summer of 1781, the American commander had not seriously contemplated anything but a concerted attack on Sir Henry Clinton in New York. From the day, however, that De Grasse arrived in the Chesapeake, and notified the American and French commanders that he would take his hope no further northward, it required no great strategist to perceive that the land forces must co operate in Virginia, if at all. From that moment the objective point of Washington and Rochambeau was palpably the force which Cornwallis, in obedience to Clinton's orders, had collected at Yorktown. Cornwallis, on his part, remained justified in remaining on the peninsula, because he counted on the English fleet, and neither then, nor before, nor afterward, could any Englishman have supposed it possible that an Admiral seeing the armament which Graves controlled would have acknowledged himself beaten on the sea by Frenchmen till half of his ships were sunk.

In view of these facts, it becomes us in this great celebration at Yorktown, to render our French visitors the honors they deserve, for the event commemorated is more truly and emphatically a French than an American achievement.

Before the advent of instant communication, printed materials were one of the most common ways to spread political ideas or propaganda.

Divisions among the colonial political leaders made themselves known when those leaders met for the Second Continental Congress, shown here.

was lawyer, politician, and American Revolution veteran Alexander Hamilton.

The First Administration and the Birth of Partisanship

Many things Hamilton and the Federalists wanted became part of the new government, with some major concessions to the anti-Federalists, who wanted states to retain influence and power. In foreign policy, Federalists wanted the nation to be neutral in a war that France and England were waging, and they generally favored peaceful relations with Britain.

Opposing them were the anti-Federalists. One was Patrick Henry, who sat out the Constitutional Convention entirely because he and other anti-Federalists feared too much central power in the hands of rulers, including the new federal government envisioned by Hamilton. As the Federalists themselves united into a true party, the anti-Federalist true believers formed what would later become the Republican Party. Foremost among Hamilton's political rivals was one of the most powerful and influential Founding Fathers and statesman, Thomas Jefferson.

Hamilton, Jefferson, and Washington: A Rivalry

A general and war hero, statesman George Washington was among

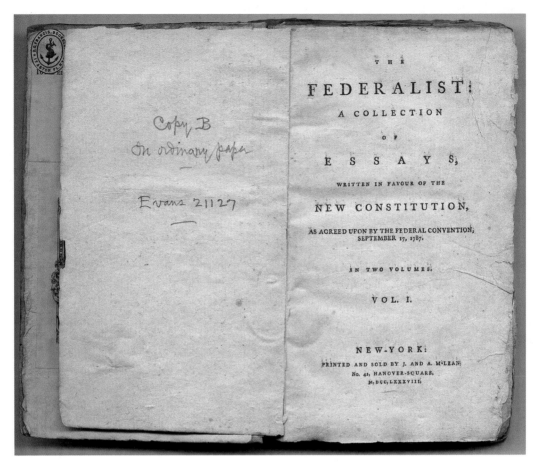

The Federalist Papers, *a collection of 85 essays and articles, were written to convince people to vote for the ratification of the U.S. Constitution.*

America's most respected figures and a natural candidate for the first president of the United States. He remained officially nonpartisan, but personally, Washington leaned toward the Federalist party. Washington had a history with Alexander Hamilton, who had served as an aide-de-camp, or assistant, and major part of Washington's inner circle during the war.

When he picked Hamilton to become the first secretary of the treasury,

Washington did so not solely due to Hamilton's beliefs and policies, which Washington agreed with. It was also because Hamilton had shown himself to be a competent administrator. At the same time, Washington selected Thomas Jefferson as his secretary of state.

Hamilton and the Federalist Party

One common political argument in this period dealt with fiscal issues—

First president George Washington tried to remain impartial when it came to the division between Federalists and anti-Federalists, but he leaned toward federalism in his own positions and beliefs.

Competing Secretaries

Personality and policy beliefs eventually came between Alexander Hamilton and Thomas Jefferson. President Washington may also have fueled the fires by seeming to make each man believe that their cabinet position was the most important in his administration. As Yale History Professor Joanne B. Freeman wrote,

> Hamilton became Secretary of the Treasury, convinced that he was a sort of Prime Minister; he often referred to "my administration." And Jefferson, as he boasted to Madison, believed that he was being put in charge of all of the domestic affairs of the nation. Obviously, this led each man to view the other as an intrusive busy-body consistently reaching beyond the bounds of his office.[1]

1. Joanne B. Freeman, "Jefferson and Hamilton, Political Rivals in Washington's Cabinet," MountVernon.org, accessed on January 30, 2018. www.mountvernon.org/george-washington/the-first-president/washingtons-presidential-cabinet/jefferson-and-hamilton-political-rivals.

that is, having to do with economic policies and government revenues from taxes. Hamilton quickly took steps in 1790 to build the economic structures that would help the government run well and hopefully thrive. One step was funding the national debt with taxes to pay it. This was the war debt of the individual states, which the U.S. government would take on. The debt was in the form of public securities, which were really I.O.U.'s promised by these local and state government banks and other institutions. Many had been sold back and forth at huge discounts, but Hamilton's idea was to pay their face value in full. This would let

people know that the U.S. government was serious and stable, generating confidence.

Hamilton advocated for a charter for a national bank, patterned after the Bank of England. The Bank of the United States motion passed Congress. Hamilton's supporters agreed it would greatly help regulate the new currency of the American dollar, first issued in 1785. Many of the powers Hamilton used were those he considered the constitutionally implied powers of the government. Hamilton cited Article I, Section 8, Clause 1 of the Constitution, a section often referred to as the General Welfare Clause, as meaning that the federal government's right to spend what it gained from taxation was very broad: "The Congress shall have Power To lay and collect Taxes, Duties, Imposts and Excises, to pay the Debts and provide for the common Defence and general Welfare of the United States; but all Duties, Imposts and Excises shall be uniform throughout the United States." His further rationale that Congress could set up a national bank in the first place drew from the Necessary and Proper Clause of the Constitution, which reads, "To make all Laws which shall be necessary and proper for carrying into Execution the foregoing Powers, and all other Powers vested by this Constitution in the Government of the United States, or in any Department or Officer thereof."[1]

If it were simply what the Constitution literally said that decided the issue, there would have been little conflict. However, Hamilton and his opponents interpreted the constitution differently. Hamilton felt they should strengthen the government and nation itself. He needed support for his ambitious programs within Washington's cabinet, in Congress, and in other influential circles. It was these supporters who would officially form his Federalist Party.

In addition, Hamilton was not above using his position in the Treasury Department to his advantage. The department's hundreds of employees formed a major portion of his support, and these treasury agents made local connections. What began as a local faction in the capital spread elsewhere. This was helped by Hamilton's own marriage years earlier in 1780 to Elizabeth Schuyler, a daughter of an American Revolution war general and member of one of the most political and richest families in New York State. Hamilton's network would quickly grow into an actual party. This generated controversy, because many people believed that his policies would unfairly enrich well-off citizens in the northeast, especially those in Hamilton's own social circles.

Opposing Hamilton

Hamilton's critics and opponents included his rival Thomas Jefferson and future president James Madison, then a member of the House of Representatives for Virginia. Jefferson and Madison especially opposed the government chartering a national bank, believing that Congress doing so would be unconstitutional. In addition, they believed it would unfairly benefit merchants and speculators.

They also opposed Hamilton's plan of a national mint to make coins and other currency. They believed that these measures could make the government too powerful, especially compared to the states, hurt local banks, and favor the northern states over southern ones. Madison believed the plan for war debt would also leave too much of the government influenced by the ultra-wealthy. This group, which Jefferson referred to as a "corrupt squadron of paper dealers"[2] in a letter to Washington in May 1792, would also receive a financial advantage from the debt repayment. Madison and

Jefferson felt that Hamilton's plans were a surefire road to tyranny and would create a new kind of monarchy. Instead of a royal family, the tyrants would be wealthy elites. It would usher in, as Madison said, "a misguided imitation of England's monarchical practice."[3]

Congress did pass versions of all of Hamilton's proposals. Washington sought the advice of both Hamilton and Jefferson, among others, on whether he should sign them into law, and he eventually did so. Madison and Hamilton, once close colleagues and friends, became bitter political rivals. Despite leaning Federalist in his beliefs, Washington did his best to calm both sides. One compromise that was included to sweeten the deal for southerners, who mostly opposed the national bank, was to build the new nation's capital in the agricultural South, along the banks of the Potomac River in Virginia. The creation of Washington, D.C., was one of the earliest legislative compromises.

Choosing Sides

Debate was quickly replaced by partisan anger and bitterness. Madison even referred to his former confidante Hamilton as a tory (an American supporter of the British during the American Revolution), a stinging and personal insult to someone who had fought against the British in the American Revolution.

In 1792, the faction led by Madison and Jefferson became known as the Republicans, named for their political philosophy, republicanism. Republicanism, among many other things, was opposed to monarchy and believed in liberty; inalienable individual rights; strong civic virtue of the citizens, including voting and self-government; and a balance of power in government that would not allow any individual branch to have more influence than the others. Jefferson and others admired the republicanism of the French Revolution that began in 1787 and had overthrown France's monarchy.

For them, Hamilton threatened the Constitution itself. Jefferson was particularly opposed to the idea of a national bank, favoring what many have referred to as a "strict interpretation" of the Constitution. Unless the Constitution explicitly called for something to exist or to happen, then it was not really permissible. Such an interpretation is sometimes also referred to as a "strict constructionist" one. In contrast, the Hamiltonians believed in a "loose interpretation."

In addition, the Hamiltonian program favored a strong federal government, especially strong executive (that of the president and his cabinet) and judiciary (the Supreme Court) branches. Hamilton respected educated, competent elites, favoring lifetime government appointments for talented administrators. He was not in favor of allowing the general public to have significant influence on decision-making and sometimes compared too much democracy to the rule of the mob.

The Republicans favored states' rights. Jeffersonian philosophy held up the legislature as perhaps the most democratic institution. Representatives were elected directly by the people, whose will should prevail. While Jefferson was a very wealthy plantation owner and slaveholder, he thought of himself as a champion of the small farmer and the common man.

The Election of 1796

The elections of 1788 to 1789 and 1792 were uncontested, and George Washington won both nearly unanimously. The race of 1796, however, was the first U.S. election that was contested and the first in which political parties were decisive. Each side had spent the previous years building passionate support for its policies and ran candidates at every level of government: national, state, and local.

The choice was clear to voters and the politicians themselves. The Federalists strongly supported Washington's vice president, Founding Father and statesman John Adams. They considered themselves to be the party of a strong national government and believed their opponents' policies would create chaos and disorder. The Federalists' strongest base of support was New England.

Opposing them were the Republicans, also known as the Jeffersonian Republicans and the Democratic-Republicans—a name that their critics used in speeches and newspaper stories, but which they later adopted. Their champion and candidate was Thomas Jefferson. Most of his support, and that of the other Democratic-Republicans, came from southerners, especially farmers.

The election was a close one. Acting as representatives of the voters, electors cast their votes for the candidates. There were rallies, newspaper editorials, and attack articles published, and leaflets were distributed. Apart from a Democratic-Republican rival of Alexander Hamilton's named Aaron Burr, the main candidates refrained from campaigning. This would remain the case for the next few decades.

Hamilton, who disliked Adams, angered many in both factions by trying to go behind the scenes to deny Adams a victory, but he failed in his attempts. Adams won 71 electoral votes, and Jefferson received 68. Jefferson was voted in as Adams's vice president, and the two took office March 4, 1797, the only time a president and vice president from opposing tickets were inaugurated together.

End of the Century: The John Adams Administration

The new administration was split between the two parties. Adams was moderate compared to Hamilton, who had resigned as secretary of the treasury in 1795 but continued to push his economic programs via allies in Adams's cabinet and government at large.

Meanwhile, tensions arose over foreign policy. The Federalists were loyally pro-British, while the Democratic-Republicans favored the French, and the two nations were then at war. The Jay Treaty, which settled many arguments and issues between the United States and Britain, angered both France and its stateside supporters. However, attempts by French foreign ministry agents to solicit bribes from U.S. representatives turned into a major scandal called the XYZ Affair.

America was soon engaged in an unofficial conflict with France, in which France seized American ships in the Caribbean Sea and elsewhere. The United States responded with retaliatory attacks in what became known as the Quasi-War. Many Americans turned against France, and Adams helped modernize and expand the U.S. military to prepare for an actual war.

Anti-French sentiment and pro-war attitudes soon led the Federalist-controlled Congress and President Adams to sign into law measures that seemed unthinkable only a few years prior. The Alien and Sedition Acts, passed in 1798, gave the government authority to deport foreigners it deemed threatening, made immigration tougher, and enacted stricter voting requirements for immigrants. The main targets of these laws were the French and the Irish, who were thought to be sympathetic to the French.

Adams's critics felt that the sedition part of these laws was extreme. This criminalized public dissent, or differing opinions, of government policies, including any writings or speech that criticized it. More than 20 journalists who harshly condemned the laws and the Federalists were arrested, and some were even jailed.

The entirely Federalist Supreme Court of the time had little incentive to attack these laws as unconstitutional. Meanwhile, James Madison and Jefferson convinced state legislators in states such as Kentucky and Virginia to reject these laws as illegal within their borders. This lined up with Republicans' strong belief in states' rights, but it also threatened to bring the federal government into conflict with the states and others who condemned its policies. The schism, or division, between Federalists and the Democratic-Republicans escalated.

A Watershed Year: The Election of 1800

In the election year of 1800, the first of the new century, Federalists launched a vicious assault on Jefferson, and the Democratic-Republicans fought back just as aggressively. Newspapers favorable to each side issued attacks back and forth. Jefferson was attacked as a radical and even an anti-Christian. The Federalists hoped to maintain strong federal authority and continue their economic programs, while the Democratic-Republicans wanted to overturn what they saw as Federalist abuses of power.

A strange provision in the voting process made the 1800 presidential election unusual. Jefferson beat Adams in electoral votes, 73 to 65. However, Aaron Burr, running as Jefferson's vice president, also received 73 electoral votes. This was because, until 1804, when the system was changed via the adoption of the 12th Amendment, electors all cast 2 votes, 1 for each candidate they thought would be the best choice for president. This was regardless of who was running for which office.

When Jefferson and Burr tied, the contest was then constitutionally decided by a vote in the House of Representatives.

Ten state congressional delegations went for Jefferson, four chose Burr, and two chose no one. Thomas Jefferson was the new president and the first peacefully elected leader to oust an incumbent, both in the United States and worldwide.

The Democratic-Republicans also made huge advances against Federalists in the House and the Senate. The historic election ushered in a new Jeffersonian era of politics, with the Democratic-Republicans dominating government for some time after. The Jeffersonians also converted many former Federalist supporters to their side. Artisans and craft workers, along with city dwellers, turned away from Adams and supported Jefferson.

The Jeffersonian Era

The new century began with Thomas Jefferson at the helm of the executive branch. He rolled back many of the Federalist policies and legislation he found misguided and abusive, and he governed with a belief in the will of the people and majority rule as guiding principles. He canceled certain federal taxes but still paid off government debt. He also tried to make peace with the Federalists in his inaugural speech, and the cabinet members he appointed were moderate Democratic-Republicans, rather than loyal anti-Federalists.

One important symbolic compromise between factions had been the relocation of the capital to the site of modern-day Washington, D.C., which had only several thousand residents at the time. The former president, Adams, had lived briefly in the newly constructed building that became known as the White House, but Jefferson was the first one to spend his full presidency there.

Democratic-Republican Thomas Jefferson (shown here), the third president of the United States, was a major rival of Alexander Hamilton and the Federalists.

The First Party System

The Democratic-Republicans would win several elections in 1804, when Thomas Jefferson was reelected to the presidency. His successor, James Madison, would win the contests in 1808 and 1812. After the United States was able to fight off the British again in the War of 1812, the Federalist Party began to fade from power and eventually disappeared. Their opposition to the war had hurt them, and the Democratic-Republicans dominated. This era of relative national unity, marked by a lack of party politics, became known as the Era of Good Feelings. The new president elected in 1816, James Monroe, won by a landslide, and he was reelected again in 1820, this time without any serious opposition. This stretch of time from 1792 through 1824, marked by the Federalists vying for power with the Democratic-Republicans, is referred to by some historians as the First Party System.

Chapter Two

DEMOCRATS AND WHIGS

In the 1820s, the nation was still young. It had more than doubled in size and population since the colonial era. Westward expansion added new territories and states to what was sometimes called the Union and caused massive conflict with Native Americans who were forced from their lands. Meanwhile, industrial growth, technological developments, and dizzying economic changes transformed America. Looming always in the background was America's "original sin:" the continued enslavement of more than 2 million people, out of a total population of more than 12 million people according to the 1830 United States Census.

The Rise of Andrew Jackson

Andrew Jackson rode a wave of popularity to political power during a time of national change. At the time, he appealed to everyday, common people. His views on marginalized groups were common for the time period, thus making him a popular president; however, his views are seen as harmful and controversial today. Jackson's rise was also in part due to the democratization of voting. In early U.S. history, many states had property requirements for voting. By the late 1820s, more and more states had abandoned these rules or created legislation to eliminate them. A growing population also meant that the old system of electors deciding elections faded away in some cases. Instead, direct votes by thousands and millions now decided many political races. Large portions of the population could now vote, and politics in this era changed to appeal to these demographics.

Democratization only applied to white men, though. White women and most African Americans remained marginalized. New York and some

Andrew Jackson, the hard-charging military hero, shook up American democracy.

other states technically gave former slaves voting rights but still forced them to maintain property requirements. In New York City, for example, it was possible to have a tiny handful of wealthy free black voters among a larger population of thousands who could not cast a ballot. Nationwide, new laws prevented free black citizens from voting where they once were able to during the colonial era.

Andrew Jackson, born in the colonial Carolinas, became an orphan at age 15 during the American Revolution, and later became a lawyer, landowner, and slaveholder. He married and became the first congressman from Tennessee and then a senator. The hot-tempered Jackson was prone to brawling and arguments, and he eventually became a militia leader. He grew famous for his brutal military campaigns against the Native Americans in the early 19th century and later became a major general in the U.S. Army. It was one tremendous victory in the War of 1812's Battle of New Orleans that made Jackson one of the most revered military heroes of his time, perhaps second only to George Washington. His incredible popularity poised him to seek the presidency in 1824.

"The Corrupt Bargain" and Its Consequences

The First Party System had ended by 1824. No Federalist would seek the presidency that election year, while the Democratic-Republicans had four hopefuls. No single candidate won a majority of the vote. The leading candidate turned out to be Andrew Jackson, who earned 99 electoral votes. John Quincy Adams, the son of former president John Adams and secretary of state for President Monroe, trailed with 84. William H. Crawford received 41 votes, and Henry Clay received 37.

Because no candidate won a majority of the votes, the House of Representatives was forced to choose between the top three candidates according to the 12th Amendment—Jackson, Adams, and Crawford. This proved to be bad luck for Jackson, because Clay was the speaker of the House of Representatives and disliked Jackson. Clay, who himself had come in fourth in the presidential vote, worked behind the scenes to have the House select Adams. Adams then picked Clay to become his secretary of state, a position the ambitious Clay greatly desired, perhaps eyeing a future presidential run.

Jackson's supporters, who disliked elites, felt that their candidate had been deceived. They called Adams's win "the corrupt bargain," considering it a symptom of a corrupt system. A likely rematch loomed for 1828. Adams, Clay, and Jackson were all Democratic-Republicans, but that party would soon be split apart.

Jacksonian Democracy: A Party Split in Two

The second showdown of Jackson and Adams in 1828 was another turning point election. Adams favored heavy

Martin Van Buren: Political Machine Pioneer

From the ashes of the First Party System came a new era. Democratic-Republicans had been warring within their own party for some time. They had embraced much of the economic ideas of the Federalists. Party politics became broader. Politicians became more attuned to public opinion.

Martin Van Buren believed in Jeffersonian democracy and was a talented politician, known for creating one of the first effective political machines. Van Buren's Albany Regency controlled New York State government from 1822 to the late 1830s. A political machine was an organization that provided employment and social services to citizens in exchange for their votes. Political machines existed nationwide. Many were accused of corruption, but others helped cities run more efficiently at a time before widespread government social services.

Van Buren was elected to the U.S. Senate in 1821 and was elected New York's governor in 1828. He did much to reorganize the Democratic-Republican Party and build its power, in particular by gaining endorsements and support from newspapers, which had exploded in number. While modern news can hardly claim to be 100-percent objective, those of Van Buren's time barely pretended to be impartial news sources. Rather, they were blatant propaganda (information of a misleading or biased nature to publicize a certain point of view or political cause) tools. Van Buren and his followers used them to spread the Democratic-Republican platform. This kept party members far and wide in line with what its leaders desired. In addition, the papers won converts to their cause and publicized political campaigns and important legislation.

Martin Van Buren was one of the first American politicians to create an efficient political machine in his home state of New York.

federal government involvement in the economy, scientific research, and university development, but his ideas rarely got off the ground. He refused to actively campaign for reelection, reportedly saying, "If the country wants my services, she must ask for them."[4] Adams's public statements often soured the common man on him. He seemed to them a throwback to the elites of the early 1800s. Meanwhile, Jackson's candidacy electrified them. Voter turnout doubled from 1824, and Jackson easily beat Adams, who followed in his father's footsteps as a one-term president.

While tailored a bit differently for his times, Jackson's message was familiar: Elites had led America astray, including those associated with the Second Bank of the United States, such as Adams and Clay. The bank was wildly unpopular among western land speculators and farmers, both major voting blocs of Jackson's.

After Adams's loss, his supporters split from the party entirely, became the opposition, and confronted the Jacksonians on a variety of issues. They became known as the National Republicans around 1830. Among these were Henry Clay, Jackson's longtime adversary, and Daniel Webster, a respected courtroom lawyer, congressman, and senator. Jackson's supporters would now be known simply as the Democrats. Despite many changes over nearly two centuries, the Democratic Party still remains the oldest continuously active political party in the Western world.

The Jacksonian Democrats came to be identified with certain values. They opposed elites and what Jackson regarded as their special privileges, and they positioned themselves as pro-farmer and pro-worker. Jackson distrusted Congress and employed the presidential veto (rejection of a proposal or decision) more often than any of his predecessors.

Jackson's history of brutal suppression of Native American resistance to being thrown off their lands would resurface in his arguably even more horrific policies of Native American removal. He received little resistance, however, from white Americans moving westward. Jackson's stance was to remove all Native Americans from the vast territories secured by Jefferson and others and offer inexpensive land, and lots of it, to U.S. settlers. Among Jackson's legacies, Native American removal and resettlement remains the most troubling.

A Jacksonian Landslide

The election of 1832 was the first where parties used conventions to nominate their candidates. Both the Democrats and the National Republicans held their conventions in Baltimore, Maryland, where Jackson received an overwhelming majority of the vote to become his party's candidate again. Meanwhile, Henry Clay was picked to run by the National Republicans.

A main issue of the election, besides Jackson's appeal over Clay on a personal level, was the question of the

BORN TO COMMAND.

OF VETO MEMORY.

HAD I BEEN CONSULTED.

KING ANDREW THE FIRST.

Political cartoons, such as this one mocking Andrew Jackson, have been an important tool used by members of all political parties to criticize leaders.

Second Bank of the United States. Jackson was determined to destroy it, as he thought it benefited only elites, while Clay favored granting it a new charter. Congress had approved an early renewal of its original charter—due to expire in 1836—but Jackson vetoed it. Jackson also distrusted the bank's president, Nicholas Biddle, who he saw as being in collusion with Clay and an enemy of the people. The controversy became known as the Bank War, and it dominated much of his time in office. Voters reelected Jackson to his second term by an overwhelming majority in both electoral votes and the popular vote.

Rise of the Whigs

The Second Party System, ushered in with the Adams-Jackson split, hit full swing when the National Republicans were resurrected in the 1830s with a new name and new allies. They mixed some classic Federalist positions with newer policies and ideas they felt could compete with Jackson's populism. The Whig Party, formed in 1834, took its name from a British party that was anti-monarchical, or opposed to the king. In the American context, this signaled to many their disdain for Jackson, whom they nicknamed "King Andrew."

Technology improved, much of the United States continued to industrialize, and businesses and localities built canals that promoted trade and opened wide areas that were previously inaccessible. Trade flourished, settlers moved west, and businesses boomed.

The Whigs believed in government developing the American economy, using the banking system and direct investments. Clay, John C. Calhoun, and Adams, all prominent Whigs, favored these policy approaches, called the American System. This meant supporting high tariffs; taxes on land sold by the federal government to settlers, which would go to states and the federal government; and a host of social and government reforms. Whigs wanted internal improvements, including roads and canals, to be paid for by tariffs and taxes.

They drew support and voters on a variety of issues. Some opposed Jackson and his Democrats for different reasons: his attacks on the Second Bank of the United States; his ignoring of Supreme Court decisions and overreaching his constitutional powers; his breaking of Native American treaties; and much more. Whigs' social policies included improving public education, prison reforms, banning the death penalty, and temperance (the fight to curtail the abuse and consumption of alcohol). The Whigs were not loyal abolitionists, but far more people opposing slavery joined their party than the proslavery Democrats.

Democrats often painted the Whigs as out of touch elitists, but there was as much propaganda as truth to this. The Whigs did relatively well with rich, poor, and middle-class voters. Overall, most wealthy urban dwellers voted Whig, as did many in boom towns. The

Democrats drew more voter support from the poor, workers, frontiersmen, and Catholics.

The Whigs tried to make their mark early on. Martin Van Buren, a skilled politician and Jackson's vice president, was the Democrats' pick for president in the 1836 presidential election. The Whigs fielded several candidates against him, including William Henry Harrison, Hugh L. White, Willie Person Magnum, and Daniel Webster. Van Buren easily beat them, running on Jacksonian democracy. Harrison, a veteran of the Indian Wars and the War of 1812 like Jackson, won enough votes to guarantee him another shot at the presidency down the line.

Vying for Power

Clay felt it was his due to finally ascend to the presidency, but the Whigs worked together to nominate Harrison in 1840 instead. When a Democrat mocked Harrison as someone as likely to sip hard cider in front of a log cabin as he would be to inhabit the White House, the Whigs ran a "log cabin and hard cider" campaign, where they held cider-fueled rallies for Harrison. Van Buren seemingly lacked Jackson's ability to appeal to the common person. Van Buren's administration also suffered a setback when the Panic of 1837 hit. Problems with land speculation in the western frontiers and declines in the price of land, cotton, and other issues set off a financial crisis and recession in the United States that lasted until the mid-1840s. That, and hard cider, seemed to make the crucial difference. The popular vote was close, but it was an electoral landslide for Harrison. The Whigs were finally in power. It was small consolation to Harrison, however, the oldest president elected up to that point: He died of pneumonia only 31 days after being inaugurated, and his vice president, John Tyler, was sworn in to replace him.

Tyler's unexpected rise hurt the Whigs. He was a former Democrat and agreed with many of their policies, but he had abandoned them because he thought Jackson had abused his presidential powers. He angered fellow Whigs when he opposed reestablishing the national bank. Despite some accomplishments, he failed to attract much support and became a man without a political party. The Democrats did not warm to him, and the power would soon shift back to them in the election of 1844.

The Democrats Rise Again

Clay once again ran for the Whig side, this time against the early Democratic front-runner Van Buren. However, Jackson and other influential Democrats blocked Van Buren's nomination. James K. Polk, former governor of Tennessee, was chosen instead. Polk, as a dark-horse candidate—unexpected and little known before the convention—would ruin a plan created by Van Buren and Clay, which was their agreement to downplay and oppose annexation of

This Whig election banner depicts the party's presidential candidate for the 1844 election, Henry Clay (left), and vice presidential candidate Theodore M. Frelinghuysen (right).

This campaign ribbon for James K. Polk proclaimed him to be the "people's choice" for president in the 1844 election. His pro-Texas stance is highlighted on the ribbon.

Texas as a new state. Many Americans, including politicians, were growing divided on slavery, and if Texas was admitted, it would likely become a slave state. Jackson had mentored Polk, who favored annexation. Van Buren had opposed it, and so did Clay (who owned slaves) because it threatened national unity.

Tyler tried to run as an independent, resurrecting the name Democratic-Republicans for his own party. Independent candidates sometimes form their own party or simply run under their own names, but his campaign fizzled. Clay believed he could win if Polk and Tyler both ran: They would split pro-annexation voters. Democrats and Polk ran on an expansionist program. The idea that the United States deserved to take over throughout the American continents became known as Manifest Destiny. Clay flip-flopped on the anti-annexation stance, and although he did not change his core position, Clay's changing viewpoints on annexation are believed to have cost him votes. Polk eked out a tiny victory in the popular vote (barely a 40,000-vote difference).

Tyler actually signed a joint congressional resolution annexing Texas three days before Polk took office in 1845. It would fall to Polk to handle the fallout from the annexation, which included a looming war with Mexico over the territory. America would win the war after capturing

Mexico City, the capital. This would win Texas for the United States, along with a great deal of other territory that Mexico ceded to it, and the war would end in February 1848, just before the next presidential election.

Although Polk, a one-term president, chose not to run for reelection, he actually fulfilled all of his inaugural promises, including reestablishing the independent treasury, the system for managing America's money supply outside the national and private banks. This was a measure to prevent panics and inflation. Polk also reduced tariffs, which stimulated trade. Finally, he settled a dispute with the British over the Oregon Territory, gaining the land that now makes up the present-day states of Oregon, Washington, and Idaho. Mexico gave up one-third of its territory to the United States due to Polk's negotiations, which included present-day New Mexico, Arizona, Utah, Nevada, and California.

Slavery, Compromise, and Division

The issue of slavery became more controversial and divisive, and neither major party could avoid it during the 1848 election. General Zachary Taylor, whose forces helped beat Mexico, did not have political experience, but the Whigs nominated him due to his public popularity.

The Democratic candidate, Lewis Cass of Michigan, tried to split the difference on slavery. Would new territories to the Union be admitted as slave states or free states? Cass's popular sovereignty stance declared that each new territory would decide for itself. This solution seemed to anger both pro- and antislavery forces. It also alienated northern Democrats, who split from their party.

These voters then joined the Free-Soil Party, founded that year as a single-issue party that opposed slavery in western territories. It also embraced the support of some antislavery Whigs and another minor antislavery party, the Liberty Party. The Free-Soil Party ran Van Buren for president. Van Buren's campaign only squeezed 10 percent of the popular vote, with Taylor winning 47 percent to Cass's 42.5 percent. Free-Soil's 291,501 votes helped defeat the Whigs in their last-ever presidential race. The threat of southern secession—that southern slave states would leave the United States and form their own country—was real and growing. With little political experience, Taylor wanted to keep the peace but did little to accomplish this.

Instead, the job fell to Calhoun, Clay, and Webster. California was to enter the Union as a free state, upsetting the current balance of 15 slave and 15 free states. Calhoun was a Democrat and lifelong advocate for slavery. Webster, a northerner from Massachusetts, opposed extending it. Clay hoped to bring the two sides to a compromise, which he succeeded in doing with the Compromise of 1850.

Under the terms of the agreement, California entered the United States as a free state, all states and the Federal government would return escaped slaves under the Fugitive Slave Act, and other territorial issues were resolved. President Taylor refused to support the compromise, but he died 16 months into his term. His successor, Millard Fillmore, signed several bills that made up the proposal. This effort would keep the Union together for another 10 years, but time was ticking for a final reckoning on slavery in the United States.

Chapter Three

REPUBLICANS AND DEMOCRATS

The Compromise of 1850 was considered a heroic legislative effort that preserved the Union, but it had done so just barely. It would cause disruptions for both major parties and lead to the end of one. It would also, however, inspire the birth of another major political party.

The Decline of the Whigs

In 1852, "a Northern man with Southern principles,"[5] Franklin Pierce, a relatively unknown senator from New Hampshire, ran on the Democratic ticket. Southern Democrats hoped Pierce would guarantee slavery's existence for some time. Pierce thought abolitionists were dangerous and had supported the Compromise of 1850. Northern Democrats, especially in New England, were wary of Pierce.

Mexican-American War veteran Winfield Scott ran on the Whig ticket. At this time, the Whigs were falling apart. Their party platform angered many supporters because of its proslavery elements. Scott generally ignored the issue during the campaign. Many Whigs sat out the election. Scott was defeated by Pierce across the board in a tremendous blow to the Whigs.

While there were some antislavery Democrats, the Whigs were bitterly divided on it. Northern party members thought the Compromise of 1850 was a failure. Antislavery forces from all parties hated President Pierce's strict enforcement of the Fugitive Slave Act. When slaves escaped from the South, law enforcement and bounty hunters everywhere were empowered to bring them back by force. Anyone interfering in their capture could be punished, too.

The Compromise of 1850 was little more than a bandage on a gaping wound. Settlers flocked to the new western territories in the early 1850s; however, a decision

This campaign banner shows Franklin Pierce as a Democratic presidential candidate. Although he was from the North, he appealed to the interests of those in the South.

still had to be made about whether to admit the new states that made up the area then known as Nebraska Territory (modern-day Kansas and Nebraska). Southerners did not want to permit these territories to be officially organized, because the Missouri Compromise of 1820 had banned slavery above the geographic line of the 36°30′ parallel. A struggle over whether to admit these territories could lead to terrible unrest.

Democratic senator Stephen A. Douglas of Illinois hoped to strike another compromise by pushing a bill into Congress. Douglas's bill would divide the territory into two units known as Kansas and Nebraska. Settlers of these territories would decide the slavery questions for themselves via their legislatures. After a bitter struggle, the South declared victory when President Pierce signed the measure, called the Kansas-Nebraska Act.

Antislavery sentiment had reached critical mass among many Democrats and even more Whigs. The act is considered one of the most important causes of the American Civil War that would ignite in the coming years.

Rise of the Republicans

Outraged northern Democrats fled, leaving the regional, proslavery faction of the South. The Whigs splintered. Their most important leaders, Clay and Webster, both passed away in 1852. A notable meeting in early 1854 in Ripon, Wisconsin, followed by a gathering of about 10,000 near Jackson, Michigan, gave birth to the Republican Party. The party name was partly credited to New York newspaperman Horace Greeley, who thought of the party as a restoration of original American values that had been neglected. They are also commonly known as the GOP, short for Grand Old Party.

Most northern Whigs opposing the Kansas-Nebraska Act flocked to the Republicans, with their southern counterparts mostly joining the Democrats. Another political faction arose at this time in the form of the Know-Nothing movement, whose anti-immigrant, anti-Catholic platform enjoyed a minor but dynamic popularity throughout the United States.

Many northerners felt antislavery was not just a major issue, but the only one. They also resented the idea that southern politicians had held the government hostage on the issue for decades. Enough was enough—slavery could not be allowed to expand.

Republicans made electoral advances. By 1855, they had a majority in the House. Party members met in Pittsburgh, Pennsylvania, in early 1856, to plan for the upcoming election. The radical wing of the Republicans was energized. Tensions were rising in places such as Kansas, where pro- and antislavery militias and supporters fought over the issue and elected separate governors and state legislators in competing elections.

As violence escalated, Republicans and Democrats both introduced

Nativists and the Know-Nothing Party

The religious component of politics would grow ever more important in the middle of the 19th century. As more immigrants arrived from countries such as Ireland and Germany to fuel the booming U.S. economy, many of them who were Catholic experienced great hostility from Protestants. The Know-Nothing movement was first a secret society that wanted to ban all immigration, which eventually grew into a small but influential party. Their name derived from their early secrecy: If someone would ask about their activities, members were told to reply that they knew nothing.

While many of the Catholic newcomers became supporters of the Democratic Party, the Protestants who feared the immigrants' growing numbers were often Whigs. This anti-immigrant movement, also known as nativism, grew quickly from the late 1840s through the 1850s. This growth was rooted in many things but was mostly due to nativists who feared the immigrants would take their jobs, as well as cultural differences and the fear this generated. In the South, the Know Nothings challenged Democrats for seats and downplayed their anti-Catholic sentiments.

RIOT IN PHILADELPHIA
JUNE 7. 1844.

Nativist riots consumed Philadelphia twice in 1844.
This illustration depicts one that occurred on July 7.

competing bills to give statehood to Kansas: The Democrats' plan called for it to join as a slave state, and the Republicans' plan called for a free state. Pro-Republican newspapers in the North published outraged stories to stoke readers' anger. When John Brown took revenge for an attack on Lawrence, Kansas, and killed five proslavery settlers at Pottawatomie Creek in the process, it made headlines in both northern and southern states. Historians estimate that attacks on both sides claimed between 60 and 200 lives before 1859 was over. More than 38 deaths occurred in 1856 alone.

The Election of 1856: A Prelude to Conflict

The brand-new Republican Party had concerns besides slavery. It favored developing a transcontinental railroad. Alongside that were the Homestead Acts, which would allow easier settling of the West. Northern business interests hoped for higher tariffs that would protect their manufactured goods from competition from imports. While many objected to slavery on a moral basis, a sizeable bloc of Republicans wanted to limit it for economic reasons. These included workers who feared competing with unpaid slave labor, especially in the new western states.

Republican leaders had little illusion about winning southern voters. However, the free North had a much larger population, and if the Republicans had solid control of the North, they could win the presidency. Republicans were willing to risk the potential for violent backlash from the South as they implemented their policies.

Proslavery Democrats selected a diplomat, Pennsylvania's James Buchanan, as their candidate for president. Challenging Buchanan was the Republicans' first-ever candidate for national office, John C. Frémont, an abolitionist, veteran, and explorer of the western United States. It became a three-way race when the Know-Nothing party, rebranded as the American Party for 1856, chose Millard Fillmore as their candidate. Buchanan squeezed out a victory but not a majority.

The Road to War

Buchanan failed to bring the North and South together and received little support from either. He was technically opposed to slavery, but he did not feel that it was unconstitutional. Perhaps Buchanan's biggest miscalculation was supporting the Lecompton Constitution. This was a state constitution drafted in 1857 by proslavery settlers in Kansas, with no input from the antislavery settlers who were greater in number and had boycotted its drafting. This soured northerners on Buchanan even more.

The election of 1860 approached. At the Democrats' nominating convention in Charleston, South Carolina, southern delegations clashed with western delegations over approaches to slavery, prompting a walkout by the southerners. Another convention in Baltimore finally nominated Stephen A. Douglas.

Political materials, such as this Nathaniel Currier lithograph depicting the campaign of 1856, often contained multiple messages for their intended audiences.

Buchanan refused to endorse him, but Douglas had recovered from the shame of igniting a minor civil conflict in Kansas. Disgruntled southern Democrats nominated their own candidate, Alabama Senator John C. Breckinridge. Democrats were now running two candidates for president, threatening to split the vote and thus potentially lose to the Republicans.

Chicago, Illinois, hosted the Republicans' convention in May. Delegates left the abolition of slavery off the party platform to try to avoid conflict with the South. New York Senator William H. Seward was an early front-runner. However, it was a talented lawyer and politician, Illinois's own Abraham Lincoln, who came out on top after multiple ballots were cast.

Attack on Charles Sumner

One longtime abolitionist from Massachusetts, Senator Charles Sumner, was part of the Republicans' radical antislavery wing. He gave a fiery speech on the Senate floor in May 1856 denouncing proslavery forces attacking antislavery supporters in Lawrence, Kansas. The speech, entitled "The Crime Against Kansas," was one of many Sumner had given in his effort to dismantle the stranglehold he felt slavery's champions held over Congress and other branches of government. He insulted South Carolina Senator Andrew Butler in the process. This prompted Butler's cousin, South Carolina Congressman Preston Brooks, to brutally attack Sumner with a cane the next day on the almost empty Senate floor. Sumner was nearly killed, and it took him three years to recover. Republicans thought of Sumner as a martyr for the cause, and it only solidified their resolve to destroy slavery. Meanwhile, Democrats considered Brooks a hero who had punished, in Brooks's own words, a "libel on South Carolina."[1]

1. "Congressional Ruffianism, Albany, New York, *Evening Journal* [Republican], May 24, 1856," Furman University, accessed on February 2, 2018. history.furman.edu/benson/docs/nyajsu56524a.htm.

SOUTHERN CHIVALRY — ARGUMENT versus CLUB'S.

South Carolinian Preston Brooks's brutal assault on abolitionist Charles Sumner in 1856 further split a tense nation on the verge of war.

Lincoln primarily stayed in Illinois, while Douglas campaigned aggressively nationwide. Lincoln spoke against the possible secession of the South, defending the Union. The two other candidates were Breckinridge and John Bell of the minor Constitutional Union Party.

Ultimately, Lincoln received only 40 percent of the popular vote but won the electoral vote. He swept almost all the northern states besides New Jersey. However, none of the Deep South voted at all for Lincoln, except for 1 percent of Virginia's population. It was an overwhelming rebuke of the Republican candidate by proslavery southerners.

Emergency meetings were called in southern state houses and among their congressional delegations. They debated furiously before many of them decided that Lincoln's election posed an immediate threat to their entire economic system and way of life. This decision led those states to secede, or formally leave the Union. South Carolina was the first to declare it had left the Union on December 24, 1860.

A Nation Divided

Four months of Buchanan's term remained after Lincoln won the Republicans their first presidency. The incumbent would do shockingly little to avert the inevitable: seven southern states left the Union by early 1861. Congress made a few attempts to reconcile with the slave states that had already left the Union, but these attempts were made in vain. Many southern legislators had either resigned or were absent from the voting.

Before Lincoln even took office that March, the United States was headed for the bloodiest chapter of its history. Four more states would secede after Lincoln's inauguration. Soldiers of the new Confederate States of America fired on Fort Sumter on April 12. The Civil War had begun. It was an incredibly destructive conflict, claiming the lives of between 752,000 and 851,000 soldiers and civilians. Many hoped it would be over quickly, but it continued for four years before the Confederacy surrendered.

Lincoln is remembered for ending slavery. His early positions on it were more moderate, even cautious. Even in wartime, a faction of the Northern Democrats continued pushing for a ceasefire and peace treaty with the South. Many Republicans ridiculed these self-styled Peace Democrats and called them Copperheads, implying they were treasonous snakes, a label many Democrats embraced.

Opposing the Copperheads in their own party were the War Democrats. Republicans accused the Copperheads of undermining the draft, which supplied the Union with troops. As the war dragged on, however, the draft grew unpopular. Lincoln and many others were more determined to preserve the Union, and ending slavery itself was a secondary issue.

However, by 1863, the president and

CHARLESTON
MERCURY
EXTRA:

Passed unanimously at 1.15 o'clock, P. M., December 20th, 1860.

AN ORDINANCE

To dissolve the Union between the State of South Carolina and other States united with her under the compact entitled "The Constitution of the United States of America."

We, the People of the State of South Carolina, in Convention assembled, do declare and ordain, and it is hereby declared and ordained,

That the Ordinance adopted by us in Convention, on the twenty-third day of May, in the year of our Lord one thousand seven hundred and eighty-eight, whereby the Constitution of the United States of America was ratified, and also, all Acts and parts of Acts of the General Assembly of this State, ratifying amendments of the said Constitution, are hereby repealed; and that the union now subsisting between South Carolina and other States, under the name of "The United States of America," is hereby dissolved.

THE
UNION
IS
DISSOLVED!

In the wake of Lincoln's election to the presidency, a wave of southern states issued official declarations of secession, many of them published by newspapers such as the one shown here.

others knew there was no turning back. In addition, the Confederacy had hoped to be recognized by foreign powers, such as Britain, as a legitimate nation. When the Union began to turn the tide and that hope died, Lincoln decided to announce his intention to free all slaves in the slave states in rebellion via the Emancipation Proclamation in September 1862. Lincoln cleverly justified it privately and later publicly as a way to instantly turn millions of slaves against the Confederacy, which had used black labor heavily in its war efforts.

Victory, Tragedy, and Reconstruction

The election of 1864 was among the most unusual in U.S. history. Most war-time leaders enjoy incredible popularity, but Lincoln came close to being voted out. The last nine presidents had only served a single term. The Peace Democrat faction ran one of Lincoln's former wartime generals, George B. McClellan, and many people expected him to win. However, the tides of war changed yet again, only days after McClellan's nomination, with explosive news about the overwhelming victories of Union general William Tecumseh Sherman in the South. Lincoln ended up winning with a sizeable popular vote total (unlike the previous election) and a huge electoral vote total.

The South finally could take no more. Confederate general Robert E. Lee surrendered his Confederate forces in April 1865, leading to the end of the war. The relief that came was short-lived, however. The white supremacist, proslavery actor John Wilkes Booth shot the president in Ford's Theatre in Washington, D.C., on April 14. Lincoln was pronounced dead on April 15, marking the first presidential assassination the United States experienced.

The task of rebuilding the Union, including the devastated South, would fall to Lincoln's vice president, Andrew Johnson. Johnson had been the sole Southern senator to not join the Confederacy. How would the North treat the South? Would the conquered population be punished? How would the now millions of emancipated slaves figure in? Answering those questions was largely Johnson's responsibility.

Constitutional amendments banning slavery, granting freedmen equal protection under the law, and granting them voting rights were quickly passed, and a process and movement called Reconstruction began. Johnson went easy on the South. He set up structures by which each state could rebuild their governments and pardoned many Southern leaders and soldiers. Southerners were also able to pass black codes, in which freed black citizens were disenfranchised and were treated only marginally better than they were during slavery. Black codes restricted freed slaves' movement. Some states restricted the property that free black citizens could own, and there were restrictions on jobs and wages.

Johnson angered Northerners, who saw that many former Confederate officials were reclaiming power. Some Northerners also disliked the black codes and how easy it was for them to be passed.

Radical Reconstruction and the Postwar Era

Infuriated by Johnson's actions, Radical Republicans swept the congressional elections of 1866, passing the Military Reconstruction Acts of 1867 and launching Radical Reconstruction. The treatment that freed black citizens received under the postwar Southern state governments outraged these Republicans. In many former Confederate states, African Americans were barred from bearing arms, hunting and fishing, using public facilities, voting, owning property, and many other activities. Many others were effectively re-enslaved, forced to work on plantations or reduced to near-slavery via sharecropping.

The Union Army occupied the South, dividing it into five zones. Under threat of gun and bayonet, black citizens were now allowed to run for political offices, vote, and join the judiciary and police forces. Union soldiers also protected black citizens. Simultaneously, Republicans aggressively pushed for the criminal prosecution of prominent secessionist military and political leaders. Southerners who had supported the Union during the war took over many government seats, alongside black citizens.

This produced a huge backlash. Johnson vetoed these measures, but congressional Republicans overrode his veto. Seen as standing in the way of justice for trying to remove Secretary of War Edwin Stanton—in charge of enforcing Reconstruction policies—Johnson was even impeached by the Republican House, but he escaped impeachment by the Senate by a single vote.

Many African Americans embraced the new system. There was cause for optimism as many were elected to state legislatures. Others even ascended to Congress. In 1871, Pinckney Benton Stewart (P. B. S.) Pinchback was the first African American to become governor of Louisiana. He took up the position of lieutenant governor when the governor died. From December 1872 to January 1873, he was acting governor while the current governor, Henry Clay Warmoth, was in the process of being impeached. Naturally, he and the more than 1,500 other African American government officeholders of the era were Republicans almost across the board.

Civil War veteran General Ulysses S. Grant, widely considered the conflict's greatest military hero, was the Republican candidate for the presidential election of 1868. Despite only a 300,000-vote difference nationally, he easily won over Democratic candidate Horatio Seymour via the Electoral College.

Grant was a member of the Radical Republican faction. His administration was known mostly for corruption

After serving as Lousiana's governor, P. B. S. Pinchback ran and won seats in both the U.S. Senate and House of Representatives. The elections were disputed, however, and Pinchback never held either office.

arising from the general's relative political inexperience. The president himself was never shown to be corrupt, nor was he perceived so by voters, but the scandals took a toll. Soon, a liberal Republican faction would rise to oppose him. Their efforts would gain steam as the election of 1872 approached.

This splinter group became an actual separate political party. Liberal Republicans believed in black political and civil rights but hoped to end Reconstruction quickly and restore self-rule. The liberal Republicans picked New York publisher Horace Greeley as their candidate. Seeing their chance to destroy their radical foe, the Democratic Party took the unusual step of endorsing and supporting Greeley's candidacy. Nevertheless, Grant was reelected easily, and the liberal Republicans dissolved after the election.

The Compromise of 1877 and the Gilded Age

New York Governor Samuel J. Tilden, a trusted reformer, ran for president on the Democratic ticket for 1876. He favored an end to Reconstruction. His Republican opponent was Ohio governor Rutherford B. Hayes. Tilden won the popular vote, but the electoral vote count was plagued by problems with vote counts in Reconstruction Republican-controlled states.

Finally, an electoral commission picked by Congress came up with the Compromise of 1877. Tilden's popular vote notwithstanding, Hayes ended up scoring 185 votes to Tilden's 184. The deal, negotiated secretly by both parties, gave Hayes the presidency. In exchange, Congress would withdraw all federal troops from the South, provide money to build southern factories, give Democrats official government posts regionally, and have a Democrat appointed to Hayes's cabinet. Hayes never quite recovered from the way he came to the office. He was always disliked by members of his own party for ceding control of the South and for his efforts to reform the civil service.

After Reconstruction, things would go from bad to worse for southern black Americans, both rich and poor. Black progress was largely reversed with local rule restored. Radical white supremacists gained the support of many regular citizens. Their terrorist organizations and secret societies, such as the racist Ku Klux Klan (KKK), caused havoc. Their reign of terror included lynching (a mob of people murdering someone, often by hanging, for an alleged offense) black citizens and otherwise conspiring to reverse and destroy the efforts of Reconstruction-era officials and governments in the South. Alongside these illegal actions, racist southern legislators established the Jim Crow laws that segregated and disenfranchised black Americans for almost a century.

Federal, state, and local leaders turned away from civil rights and Reconstruction. Instead, the nation turned its attention to pro-business, pro-industrial policies. Industry, railroads, trade, and other business activities became the new centers of power during this time, known as the Gilded Age. It was named so for the vast amounts of money the top level of industrialists and other leaders made and the power they wielded over Congress and other public and private institutions. Congress seemed to call the shots during the Gilded Age, as opposed to previous eras, when agendas were set mainly by presidents.

The Republicans would dominate in post-Civil War America with policies that were holdovers inherited from the Whig era. Meanwhile, the Democrats would maintain power in the former states of the Confederacy. Their reliance on Jim Crow and their tendency to vote together on issues of common interest was known popularly as the "Solid South."

In large cities, such as New York and Chicago, political patronage dominated. This was a system of giving out jobs and favors to those who could bring votes or vote for certain politicians in return. Corruption was rampant, and political machines dominated. The exit of Grant did not clean up the government, and bribery, favoritism, and draining public monies from the public were commonplace.

Chapter Four

THE NEW CENTURY

America became an industrial powerhouse, and its politics adapted to the influence and money that big business generated. Religious revivals, along with the temperance movement against alcohol, mass immigration, urbanization, and continued westward expansion, made America a very different country than it had been when the Civil War began. However, these phenomena also presented their own issues and inspired conflict among competing groups.

Backlash to Inequality: The Progressive Era

It was an era of fierce competition in business, dominated by a winner-takes-all mentality. Millions of laborers, many of them newer immigrants, worked long hours for low pay in often poor conditions. The booming economy also provided opportunities for millions of others to prosper. Still, millions more suffered.

Even the fortunes of the wealthy could sometimes be wiped out at a moment's notice. Between 1877 and 1893, the American economy doubled. Stock speculation made things unpredictable. Few laws regulated business, and Congress was not motivated to pass any. The Gilded Age produced business leaders who seemed larger than life and appeared to wield more power than senators, congressmen, and even presidents. Industrialists such as John D. Rockefeller, Andrew Carnegie, and Andrew Mellon led multi-million-dollar businesses in the oil, steel, and financial industries, respectively, and were sometimes known as robber barons.

THE PROTECTORS OF OUR INDUSTRIES.

General discontent with the inequality of the Gilded Age was expressed with politically charged materials that attacked the richest captains of industry of the era.

Dawn of the Fourth Party System

By the mid-1890s, the Third Party System issues such as slavery and Reconstruction gave way to a new era and new issues. Many leaders rising at the time recognized how unfair and sometimes even dangerous placing too much power in the hands of a few businessmen could be. Rockefeller and others formed trusts.

This meant that several businesses were combined in an industry sector, such as oil, where a single person or group worked to set prices or cooperate in other ways that eliminated competition and profited the owners of the trust. Businesses that competed unfairly— mainly by buying up their competitors and then charging more money—were also called monopolies.

The Rise of the Populists

From the Gilded Age on, American workers began organizing for mutual benefit and for their own economic preservation. Unions bargained with business owners and sometimes went on strike to disrupt business and achieve workers' goals, such as better wages, shorter hours, and better working conditions. Farmers organized into granges, organizations that began more as social clubs and secret societies, and then pressed state government to benefit crop prices and achieve other goals. Granges banded together, and some even formed farmers' alliances, such as the National Farmer's Alliance, commonly called the Southern Farmers' Alliance, in 1877. Some of them ran their own candidates for office who would be sympathetic to farmers' concerns. A coalition of the Farmers' Alliances, the National Grange, and the Knights of Labor organization formed in 1892 as the People's Party, also known as the Populist Party. That election year, while the Democrat Grover Cleveland became president with 5.5 million votes total over Benjamin Harrison's 5.1 million, the Populists' candidate, former Iowa congressman James B. Weaver, received more than 1 million votes.

Several movements arose in the late 19th century that would challenge pro-business politics and try to help regular people. There had been a few small third-party movements that had brought new ideas to wider audiences. An economic panic in 1893 left many people in the United States unemployed and suffering—and open to new ways of thinking.

Nebraska lawyer William Jennings Bryan was a youthful former congressman known for being a brilliant speaker. Farmers and others with debt were then pushing to end the gold standard and increase inflation, which would help many of them sell their goods more easily. Bryan believed in promoting silver coinage (called the Free Silver Movement), encouraging inflation, lowering tariffs, and supporting farmers. Democrats worked behind the scenes to enlist him as their candidate in 1896. He stunned and excited the attendees of the Chicago Democratic Convention in July in a famous speech in which he said, "We will answer their demand for a gold standard by saying to them: You shall not press down upon the brow of labor this crown of thorns, you shall not crucify mankind upon a cross of gold."[6] He also ran on the ticket of the minor Populist Party.

The dynamic speaker and politician William Jennings Bryan made a huge impact on Populist and Progressive politics at the turn of the 20th century, inside and outside the Democratic Party.

With Bryan the seeming champion of the common man, his Republican opponent, Ohio governor William McKinley, was the favored candidate of business interests, including supporters of the gold standard. A few dozen delegates who supported the Free Silver Movement walked out of the Republican convention, later supporting Bryan. Many of them hailed from western states where silver mining was booming.

The Democrats had their own mutiny with the Gold Bug Democrats. This conservative faction mirrored the Free Silver activists but favored the gold standard, a stance in opposition to their party's official platform. The incumbent president, Grover Cleveland, was one of the leaders of this faction, which styled itself the National Democratic Party and was sometimes known as the Bourbon Democrats. Others flipped to the Republicans for this election.

Bryan lost to McKinley by about 500,000 votes. While the Free Silver Movement appealed to farmers and agricultural regions, rich and poor alike in cities distrusted it. Recovery from the Panic of 1893 likely helped McKinley win. McKinley's Republican National Committee also waged a national, disciplined campaign that emphasized prosperity and painted his opponent as passionate but misguided. Business owners told workers that a vote for Bryan would result in factory closures. Furthermore, direct contributions from corporations amounted to somewhere between $3.5 and $4 million for McKinley versus a mere $600,000 raised by Bryan. Huge cash influxes went a long way toward buying newspaper and magazine ads and influencing editorials.

McKinley's extensive fundraising would set the stage for campaigning for many decades to come. However, Bryan's populism, tied to his charisma and engagement with large groups all around the country, was something relatively new, too. In addition, the old divide between North and South was vanishing and being replaced by urban versus rural and eastern versus western issues influencing election outcomes. Traditional voting blocs of the old days had shifted.

Teddy Roosevelt and the Progressive Movement

Bryan challenged McKinley again in 1900, but the Free Silver issue had fizzled. Another Democratic issue was anti-imperialism—that is, not interfering militarily or otherwise in the affairs of other nations, as the United States had recently done in its victory in the Spanish-American War. This also failed to stir winning momentum for Bryan. A relatively prosperous economy also helped McKinley.

Still, the spirit of change was in the air and not isolated to just one party. The previous year marked the death of McKinley's vice president, Garret Hobart. He was replaced by Theodore "Teddy" Roosevelt, a veteran hero of the Spanish-American War, former governor of New York, esteemed

The larger-than-life Theodore Roosevelt spoke of progressivism and its ideals. He focused on protecting consumers and protecting the wilderness in America, among other beliefs.

wildlife enthusiast, author, and all-around renaissance man (a person with many areas of knowledge or talents).

Republican officials considered Roosevelt a loose cannon. However, his popularity and charisma helped McKinley. No one predicted that an anarchist would assassinate McKinley in September 1901, six months into his second term. Suddenly, the loose cannon was president, the youngest the nation had known. His aggressive, energetic style and accomplishments made him enormously popular with common people. Like few presidents before him (such as Andrew Jackson), he distrusted elites, even though he was born into a wealthy family. Roosevelt considered himself a champion of working people and an enemy of monopolies and trusts. In 1903, he sought legislation to create a government agency to regulate business abuses, the Bureau of Corporations, which was a predecessor of the Federal Trade Commission (FTC). He called his political philosophy the Square Deal. It had three goals: protect consumers, prevent corporations from abusing their powers, and protect America's wilderness. Roosevelt stated "that the rich man should have justice, and that the poor man should have justice, and that no man should have more or less."[7]

During the 1904 campaign, the Republican was seen as the candidate of the common person. Roosevelt aggressively attacked the business trusts and personally intervened in a coal miners' strike on behalf of labor. He had even invited Booker T. Washington, the founder of Tuskegee Institute and the nation's most prominent black leader, to dinner, earning outrage from southern Democrats.

His Democratic opponent this time was the conservative Appeals Court judge Alton B. Parker. Some business leaders attempted a "Stop Roosevelt" campaign, but he proved too popular. Roosevelt scored one of the biggest wins in presidential history, beating Parker by 18.8 percent of the popular vote, a remarkable result since he did not carry a single southern state. Roosevelt used his second term to set aside millions of acres of wilderness as national parks and forests and increased protected lands by threefold during his time in office.

Roosevelt had promised not to seek a third term when he won his second. It was an unofficial tradition, as term limits had not yet been constitutionally instituted. Roosevelt had suffered politically from a Wall Street panic in 1907, and many of his own party members from the conservative wing pushed back more aggressively against his policies than they had earlier in his tenure. From a sense of duty to keep his promise, he stepped aside and named his close colleague, William Howard Taft, as his successor. His endorsement was still powerful enough to get Taft the Republican nomination for 1908.

Carrying the Progressive Torch

The Progressive wing of the Republicans felt Taft to be worthy. Meanwhile, its conservative wing had no special love for Taft or Roosevelt but would not abandon them for the opposition. William Jennings Bryan ran for the presidency for the third and last time for the Democrats.

Bryan's moment had passed, however. Roosevelt had stolen the Progressive and Populist thunder Bryan had once enjoyed. The Populist Party itself ran Tom Watson, who had gotten only 120,000 votes in 1904. This time, with Bryan drawing the more radical vote, they only got 30,000 votes and would disappear from the national political stage. Taft carried the torch without going quite as far to the Left as Bryan, striking an ideal balance for voters, and won the presidency.

Taft was no Roosevelt, however, and was pulled apart by the two wings of the Republican Party. A scandal involving Richard Ballinger, the Secretary of the Interior, damaged Taft's credibility when Ballinger was accused of helping mining interests exploit Alaska for coal. Gifford Pinchot, Roosevelt's close friend and adviser to both Taft and Roosevelt on forestry issues, attacked Ballinger and Taft publicly. Taft fired Pinchot, alienating Progressives and angering Roosevelt.

Taft would look indecisive and weak on other issues. The Payne-Aldrich Tariff Act of 1909 raised tariffs for the first time in a decade, violating an election platform promise made by the Republicans, which angered Progressives. Conservative Republicans favored it, leaving the party divided. Roosevelt returned from an overseas trip and was determined to push Taft out in 1912. He considered his protégé a traitor on his beloved conservation issues. Roosevelt was known as hotheaded, and later historians believe he was too blinded by his anger to see that Taft actually had a fine Progressive record. He had supported direct voter election of senators, a reform many had long desired. Taft had also instituted an eight-hour workday for federal employees and set up the Children's Bureau, the first federal agency designed to improve the lives of children and families.

The "Bull Moose" Party versus Republicans and Democrats

Bad blood dominated the election of 1912. Roosevelt wanted to run to punish Taft and restore his Progressive legacy, an act that some suspected was simply Roosevelt being impulsive and egotistical. Whatever his motivation, Roosevelt's proposed platform, publicized earlier that year as "New Nationalism," was among the most reform-minded of its time. It called for women's suffrage (the right to vote), health care funds for citizens, retiree pension funds, a minimum wage, and a system of workers' compensation. The former president was thwarted in his play for the Republican nomination in Chicago that year, however; Taft got the nod instead. Roosevelt was furious but determined, taking his followers to form a new organization, the Progressive Party, also known as the Bull Moose Party after characteristics of strength and toughness that Roosevelt used to describe himself.

Democrat Woodrow Wilson, the governor of New Jersey, got a last-minute endorsement from William Jennings Bryan. The race for 1912 was on. The Democrats were ecstatic about the Republican split. Wilson's own moderate reforms took aim at tariffs, as well as the banking interests and other business trusts. Wilson's platform, which he called the "New Freedom," was targeted at the common person, whether they worked in the fields or owned a small business in the city.

With Roosevelt and Taft splitting the vote of the Republicans, Wilson won an electoral vote landslide, with Socialist candidate Eugene V. Debs a distant fourth. The new president followed through on many of his campaign promises, passing banking reforms such as the Federal Reserve Act, reducing tariffs, strengthening antitrust regulations, and supporting policies that helped farmers and entrepreneurs. One of the greatest tests for Wilson and the nation loomed ahead, however, as World War I began in Europe in 1914.

Wilson and others were noninterventionist when it came to the massive conflict igniting overseas halfway through his first term. As the 1916 election approached, Wilson kept the nation out of war and wanted to maintain relations and trade with both sides, but it was uncertain how long he could do so. Many Americans were antiwar, so much so that Wilson's Democrats used "He Kept Us Out of War" as a campaign slogan. Republican Charles E. Hughes, a Supreme Court Justice, tried to attack Wilson's campaign by declaring him weak on preparedness and accusing him of being too pro-labor and anti-business. However, Wilson prevailed in a close race.

Even so, German submarines and ships had been attacking American ships in the Atlantic steadily for some time. They considered American ships breaking their blockade of Britain to be an act of aggression. These attacks escalated so much that the United States declared war on Germany in April 1917, a month after Wilson had his second inauguration. Among the few members of Congress who voted against the war were six Senators and fifty members of the House. One of those was the first female member of Congress, Montana's Jeannette Rankin, who would later be instrumental in gaining women the right to vote. America began to prepare for war, abroad and at home.

The United States and the Allies defeated Germany and the Central Powers. Wilson and other leaders attempted to obtain U.S. membership in the League of Nations, an international organization similar to today's

How They're Acting — and How They Feel

This cartoon by Clifford K. Berryman depicts what many felt to be the external and internal attitudes of the three presidential candidates during the 1912 campaign.

United Nations that would try to negotiate disagreements and prevent war. Republican Senate leader Henry Cabot Lodge was wary of joining and disdained the agreement that officially ended the war. He felt that Wilson was needlessly surrendering U.S. sovereignty to an international organization and risking its independent foreign policy.

The Roaring Twenties and the Business of America

The Republicans took back the presidency in 1920. That election year, almost 100 years of protests, activism, and sacrifice yielded victory for women's suffrage. With the ratification of the 19th Amendment on August 18, women in the United States now had the inalienable right to vote. On November 2, 1920, more than 8 million would do so across the United States.

Building on the momentum of the 1918 midterm elections, Republicans were confident they would retake the White House. Major problems, including anti-black race riots partly caused by economic troubles, made many voters want to put the war and the previous decade behind them. Ohio Senate Republican Warren G. Harding's "Return to Normalcy" campaign slogan appealed to many different voters, and he was voted in easily with Calvin Coolidge as his vice president. Only the South turned out heavily for the Democratic governor of Ohio, James M. Cox.

Harding would favor a policy that became central in the Republican platform over the next century: noninterference in business, also known as laissez-faire. Another one would be lower taxes. He was also a protectionist, meaning he favored tariffs to protect American producers.

Harding died of what is today believed to be one or more heart attacks in 1923, and Coolidge was sworn in. The former Massachusetts governor continued Harding's hands-off policies. Despite signs that an economic bubble could burst, Coolidge avoided taking action. He also was wary of passing legislation to help farmers, whose livelihoods were badly affected by a crash in agricultural prices. Nevertheless, Coolidge did not have to do much to remain popular. Otherwise, the economy seemed healthy.

Republicans were unified during the 1924 presidential race, but the Democrats were split. Al Smith, governor of New York, vied for the nomination and was popular in the Northeast but was greatly disliked in the South and West. The KKK, revived in the 1920s with millions of followers, was highly influential, especially among southern Democrats. Their presence at the Democratic convention even provoked fistfights. The KKK hated Smith because he was a Catholic. When the Democrats finally picked West Virginia politician John W. Davis, he failed to motivate voters and lost in a landslide. Progressive Party candidate

The KKK's presence at the 1924 Democratic convention, shown here, was highly controversial.

Robert M. La Follette, governor of Wisconsin, had a strong third-place showing with nearly 16.6 percent of the popular vote, after failing to get the Republican nomination over Coolidge.

Unlike the earlier Roosevelt era, the party had shifted and had little room for leftist candidates, at least nationally.

The slogan "Coolidge or Chaos" reminded the public of the relative

prosperity of the time and that they should vote to preserve it. Regarding his plans for the 1928 election, his only message to the press was, "I do not choose to run in 1928."[8] Many attributed this decision to depression following the death of his son four years earlier, but the public was genuinely surprised. It was widely believed that Coolidge could have won again.

Before the Fall: Herbert Hoover

Herbert Hoover, a Republican mining magnate and former secretary of commerce under Presidents Harding and Coolidge, hoped to continue the Republican winning streak. The Democratic challenger was again Al Smith. Smith's party's platform pressed aid to farmers, was pro-labor, and called for an end to a military occupation of the Philippines that had lasted since 1902.

Smith's position on Prohibition, or the amendment that banned the sale, manufacturing, and transport of alcohol, was problematic. While the Democratic platform did not call for repealing the amendment, Smith was known as "wet," or strongly in opposition to Prohibition. Even a vice presidential running mate who was "dry," Arkansas senator Joseph T. Robinson, did little to help Smith in the temperance-minded southern Bible Belt. His Catholicism and thick New York accent turned off these voters even more. Since the 1924 race, radio had become an important part of campaigning. Smith's usual charisma did not translate well everywhere.

In an October speech at New York's Madison Square Garden, Hoover said Republican policies had provided prosperity, giving Americans "a chicken in every pot … and a car in every backyard, to boot."[9] Hoover also spoke of rugged individualism, which is the belief that government intervention should be minimal and people could succeed on their own. Competition and the free market would bring these, Hoover declared, not a turn toward socialism. Hoover won the election in a landslide victory, although turnout for both men was tremendous.

Chapter Five

THE NEW DEAL ERA

The energy and prosperity of the Roaring Twenties would not last, and the rugged individualism of Hoover and his fellow Republicans would be put to the test in the coming years. Booming economic times had a dark underside, and a stock market bubble that had grown too large was only part of the problem.

The Crash and the Great Depression

The automobile industry and other businesses were booming, but too much money had been invested in the stock market. Many people bought products on credit instead of cash. They even bought huge amounts of stock on borrowed money. An earlier decline in agricultural markets, falling wages, and other factors made the stock and credit bubble a house of cards waiting to topple. When the stock market crashed, people began to understand how inflated stock prices were. A massive sell-off began, crashing prices quickly. The panic, which hit full speed on Tuesday, October 29, 1929, set off a downward spiral. Half of the stock market was wiped out in weeks. Soon, a run on the banks of people trying to recover savings caused a wave of bank failures and closings. This was before accounts were guaranteed by federal law.

Huge layoffs followed. The ensuing crisis, known as the Great Depression, was the worst one ever to hit America. Its shockwaves hit markets and economies worldwide, and unemployment skyrocketed. Many Americans were plunged into desperate circumstances, and bread lines and other signs of the collapse soon appeared all over the United States.

How Hoover and his party reacted to these problems became the primary political issue of the next elections in

1932. Hoover had warned his predecessors about putting the brakes on over-speculation, but he drew blame for his weak responses to the crisis. The Democratic Party began to press hard to portray itself as a supporter of the poor and unemployed masses of voters. Unemployment, by many accounts, stood as high as 25 percent. They blamed the crash on Republican laissez-faire policies.

Americans grew desperate for government help during tough times. Hoover's philosophy of rugged individualism seemed increasingly out of touch. Hundreds of thousands of Americans now gathered in makeshift cities of tents and handmade shacks, sarcastically called

The poverty and desperation of the Great Depression was blamed, fairly or unfairly, on Hoover. This attitude was reflected in the shantytowns of the era, which were nicknamed "Hoovervilles."

"Hoovervilles." The Democrats took the House in the 1930 midterms. Hoover increased federal spending in 1931, along with increased taxation. Even though he put $500 million into bank and business loans in 1931 to stimulate public works that would hire workers, it was too little, too late.

Then, a movement of World War I veterans, who Congress had promised a bonus of $1,000 in 1924—payable by 1945—demanded early payment. In June 1932, thousands ended up gathering in a shantytown near Washington, D.C., as a protest, dubbed the Bonus Army, to demand this pay. Even after the Senate rejected their demands, thousands remained. Hoover ordered the military to break up the camp and clear out the demonstration. At least two people were killed in the violence, and a stunned nation was outraged.

A Major Realignment: Roosevelt's New Deal

The 1932 election would be a major realigning election. Franklin Delano Roosevelt, the popular New York governor and fifth cousin of the Progressive former president Theodore Roosevelt, was the Democratic nominee. He promised a New Deal for Americans. This platform promised massive help for Americans in the form of money, jobs, and public works projects that would stimulate and jump-start the economy again.

Roosevelt undertook a massive tour of the United States by train and outshined Hoover as they both tried to make their case to millions more voters via radio addresses. An electoral landslide and a popular vote of 57.3 percent swept the Republicans out of power that November. Democrats also won control of the Senate on top of their House dominance. Americans had chosen government intervention over the self-help that Hoover offered.

With a sympathetic, Democrat-controlled Congress, Roosevelt went to work. He created the Federal Deposit Insurance Corporation (FDIC), which mandated that the federal government protect bank deposits of all individuals up to $2,500. This was part of the larger Banking Act of 1933, also known as the Glass-Steagall Act, which also made it illegal for banks to mingle their speculative businesses (investment banking) and the banking that average people used (commercial banking). The New Deal also included plans that helped the jobless and the homeless, provided aid to farmers, and provided funding for massive public works projects, including publicly owned power utilities such as power plants and dams. The Works Progress Administration (WPA) employed millions of Americans directly.

The economy was slow to recover, so Roosevelt and Congress passed these measures to keep people employed and spending. Those to Roosevelt's political left, such as Socialists, felt they did not

Opponents and supporters of Roosevelt and his New Deal often used newspapers and other media to express their views.

go far enough. Roosevelt is often considered a savior of capitalism, since he merely put in place safeguards to protect the most vulnerable in society and did not dismantle the system outright, a solution others sought.

These measures were wildly popular, but a hardcore group of Republicans and others soon grew to oppose them, nevertheless. Any limits on business and individual responsibility alarmed them. They believed a leftward shift would lead to full communism and hurt the bottom lines of business owners and entrepreneurs. This stance would exist in some form or another as part of the Republican platform until the present day.

Implementing much of the New Deal meant a big scale-up of the federal government. A large bureaucracy was put into place that would be repeatedly attacked by Republican challengers and administrations throughout the 20th century and still today—and even by many modern Democrats. Much of these measures aimed to protect consumers and everyday people. New agencies included the Securities and Exchange Commission (SEC), formed to regulate stock markets and agencies that loaned and helped homeowners; the Public Works Administration, which built bridges, schools, dams, parks, and more; and the National Labor Relations Board (NLRB).

The NLRB was particularly welcomed by labor activists and Socialists. It was made permanent in the National Labor Relations Act of 1935. Roosevelt's administration was the first time that the government had recognized the right of labor unions to strike and take other actions to increase wages, improve conditions, and otherwise advocate for their members. Unions that had declined in the 1920s under Republican policies bounced back tremendously. The resurgence of unions also gained Roosevelt and the Democrats more votes and support among workers. Many became Democratic Party activists and organizers, and much of the party's power from the 1930s on was rooted in the union movement.

The New Deal: Supporters and Opponents

The election of 1936 was a referendum on New Deal policies. The Depression lasted through the entire 1930s, but a majority of voters nonetheless thought Roosevelt's Democrats were on the right track. Many Americans were back at work or otherwise saw Roosevelt's policies make a positive change in their own lives. Legislation that established unemployment insurance benefits and the Social Security retirement pension system were also extremely popular.

The Republican candidate was Kansas governor Alf Landon. Landon was the only Republican elected to a governorship in 1934, an indication of how unpopular the party had become. Landon personally agreed with much of the New Deal and did little to publicly challenge it. He was reluctant to campaign hard, and his last-minute tactics of attacking Roosevelt for corruption and possibly becoming a dictator were ineffective. Another landslide victory reelected Roosevelt and had Democrats controlling the Senate. It was the biggest win for any party since 1820, an uncontested year. Even leftist voters—who criticized the New Deal for not going far enough—did not want to derail Roosevelt's efforts too much.

The New Deal brought together a new set of interest groups and voting blocs that would largely support Democratic politicians from the 1930s through the 1960s. Many members of this New Deal Coalition had different interests

The Socialist Party and Eugene Debs

Many Socialists came out of the union movement, and many continued to hold power in unions throughout the early 20th century. Eugene V. Debs made national news in 1894 when the union he cofounded in 1893, the American Railway Union (ARU), organized a strike that affected dozens of states and more than 250,000 workers and he spent 6 months in federal prison when he defied a related court order.

In 1900, Debs received about 87,000 votes as a presidential candidate for the Social Democratic Party of America. A year later, that group was folded into the Socialist Party of America. Debs ran for president again in 1904, receiving more than 400,000 votes, and in 1908, he received more than 420,000 votes. In 1912, the Socialists had their strongest showing and received more than 900,000 votes, or about 6 percent of the total vote.

The Socialists and others on the Left favored social programs to help the poor and marginalized, as well as Populist reforms that helped farmers and workers, especially labor unions. However, political repression during World War I and the 1920s, as well as other parties moving leftward, such as the Democrats, prevented the Socialists from growing. An antiwar speech landed Debs in prison again, but he ran for president while in jail in 1920, again earning more than 900,000 votes.

FOR PRESIDENT

EUGENE VICTOR DEBS

Union leader Eugene V. Debs ran for president five times as the candidate of the Socialist Party.

and worldviews but benefited somehow from Roosevelt's policies. These included black Americans, who shifted away from the Republican party; northern city dwellers, including workers, immigrants, liberals, and intellectuals; Catholics; Jewish people; labor unions and their workers; various religious and ethnic minorities; and small farmers.

World War II and After

Only a massive industrial and military buildup by the United States to support efforts to fight Germany and Japan in World War II would truly end the Great Depression. The war began in 1939, when Adolf Hitler's Germany invaded Poland before invading France and other nations, but America stayed out of the war, although it supported Britain, France, and the other Allies.

A big issue of the 1940 election was whether Roosevelt should run for a third term, which would break the 150-year tradition of a maximum 2 terms for president. Roosevelt countered that the nation was still in crisis and possibly faced another crisis overseas, sooner or later.

His opponent turned out to be Republican dark-horse candidate Wendell Willkie, a lawyer and executive. Willkie himself was an interventionist, but with the New Deal still popular (and the Republican Party itself unpopular), he attacked Roosevelt, claiming the United States was not ready for war but that Roosevelt was saying things that would force it to fight. Roosevelt countered that, if elected, he would keep America out of the war. Roosevelt won a huge electoral victory that year, but with a slimmer winning margin of just under 5 million votes, out of nearly 50 million cast.

The nation would go to war against the Axis Powers after Pearl Harbor was attacked by the Japanese on December 7, 1941. Willkie later teamed up with Roosevelt to gather support for much of the president's platform and was considered a liberal Progressive in his party. This wing of the party would diminish in the decades after the war.

Roosevelt, still popular and engaged in wartime efforts overseas and at home, faced off in 1944 against Thomas E. Dewey, the Republican candidate and governor of New York, considered a moderate and Progressive in his party. Dewey's campaign criticized corruption and inefficiencies in the New Deal. The Republicans stayed quiet on anything related to the war effort. The election was even closer than 1940, but Roosevelt prevailed for the fourth time. It was the last election where the Democrats would win the whole South. America's wartime leader would soon pass away, dying of a massive stroke in April 1945, and Harry Truman was sworn in as president.

By the end of World War II in 1945, the United States was the only power that had not suffered on the home front. Spirits were high after victory. Helping rebuild Europe, the United States would eventually enter its own most prosperous era, where millions entered the middle-class. It would also engage in a Cold War with the Soviet Union. Previously allies in World War II, the two nations faced off internationally over which system of government and which nation would dominate the globe. The Cold War would stay one of the most important issues during the postwar era.

The Postwar Era

With a few exceptions, the Democratic Party seemed to dominate in the years after World War II through the late 1960s. It controlled both houses of Congress, and both parties would favor anti-Communism as a pillar of their foreign policy.

Republicans reclaimed both chambers of Congress in 1947. Growing support for the party made them confident of presidential victory in 1948. Harry Truman ran against Thomas Dewey. Black civil rights issues were beginning to divide the Democrats. A southern delegation, angry with the party's inclusion of pro-civil rights positions in the Democratic platform, walked out of their convention and formed a splinter faction, the Dixiecrats (officially, the States' Rights Democratic Party). Division on this issue would continue to plague the party well into the 1960s. A Progressive Party campaign by Henry A. Wallace attacked Truman from the Left, too.

Media and the public at large were stunned on election night, because many had predicted Truman's defeat. A now famous *Chicago Daily Tribune* newspaper

front page proclaiming "Dewey Defeats Truman"[10] had been pre-approved before all the results were in. Truman defeated Dewey, and the Democrats retook Congress. While the Democrats held the presidency again, the coming years would test their winning combination of voting blocs, sometimes known as the New Deal Coalition.

In 1952, the Cold War was a major issue. A recession had hit the country in the early part of the 1950s, and America had intervened in the Korean War on behalf of the southern half of the country to defeat its Communist north. Now the war was in a stalemate. Truman had lost steam and declined to run again. Illinois governor Adlai Stevenson ran for the Democrats instead. Not having desired running before he was picked on the third ballot in their Chicago convention, the Progressive Stevenson was the first candidate drafted for a race since Grover Cleveland.

Republicans hoped to win their first presidential race since 1928. Northeastern and Midwestern Republicans were largely organized along two wings. The Midwesterners strongly supported Robert A. Taft, a senator from Ohio, and were isolationist conservatives. Northeastern Republicans wanted Dwight D. Eisenhower, the heroic World War II general who favored a strong international role for the United States. Eisenhower later privately assured Taft and his supporters that he would generally favor their domestic policies. With his military record, voters trusted

A victorious Harry Truman held up the infamous "Dewey Defeats Truman" newspaper headline a day after he actually won the presidency.

Eisenhower's promises to "bring the Korean war to an early and honorable end."[11] They were also ready for a change. Eisenhower won in a landslide over Stevenson.

Eisenhower represented the moderate wing of his party, even calling his particular program "Modern Republicanism." This middle-of-the-road stance favored keeping the New Deal policies of Roosevelt but not expanding them too much. They were protected from conservative Republicans who wanted to repeal them, partly because Eisenhower and others saw their mission as good practices in government. Looked at in the modern context, many of his positions align with that of present-day conservative Democrats. In Eisenhower's time, it was more common to find party members of both major parties (and some minor third parties) who were all over the political spectrum.

Little major changes happened in the United States until the late 1950s. Rather, Eisenhower's first term was marked by the end of the Korean War, increasing prosperity in America, moves by many city dwellers to the suburbs, continued anti-Communist sentiments, and a cultural and political conformity that many people still identify with the decade.

The moderate Eisenhower was able to get a Democrat-controlled Congress to work with him on many occasions, including creating the Interstate Highway System in 1956. That year, Eisenhower easily beat Adlai Stevenson once more, because of the nation's relative prosperity and the fact that many on both sides generally liked him and respected his presidency. Still, the Democrats maintained a slim majority in the Senate and a comfortable one in the House.

Eisenhower was not a fervent warrior for civil rights, but he signed moderate legislation in favor of it. On one hand, he was lukewarm toward the Supreme Court decision in the case of *Brown v. Board of Education*, which declared school segregation unlawful. However, he deployed federal forces to protect black students who were integrating Central High School in Little Rock, Arkansas, in 1957. The effort of black Americans to gain dignity, rights, and economic justice, broadcast on the young medium of television, would stir the conscience of many Americans well into the next presidency and inspire change.

The 1960s: Another Realignment

A thirst for something new and fresh marked the beginning of the new decade, and a presidential race to match that spirit would unfold in 1960. The 22nd Amendment, approved in 1951, meant that Eisenhower could not constitutionally run again, as it stated that no president shall be elected to the office for more than two terms.

A youthful and rising star in the Democratic Party, Massachusetts Senator John F. Kennedy, faced off against Eisenhower's vice president, Richard M. Nixon. Nixon was faithfully

The 1960 presidential race between John F. Kennedy and Richard Nixon was the first presidential race to unfold in a major way on television.

anti-Communist and a conservative. Kennedy also ran on an anti-Communist platform and thus stole Nixon's thunder somewhat on that front. He also said the Republicans had failed to match the Soviet Union in the race to explore space.

Television figured heavily into the election itself. A televised debate between the two men is said to have tipped the public's favor to Kennedy, due to Kennedy's energetic, youthful appearance. Because television was in black and white at the time, Nixon's deep eyes and heavy eyebrows created shadows on his face and made him look sinister. During another televised press conference, Eisenhower stumbled when asked to name a single idea of Nixon's during his own eight-year term, only joking, "If you give me a week, I might think of one."[12] Kennedy would win one of the closest elections in the nation's history and would become its youngest inaugurated and the first Catholic president. His religion had been an issue, as Democrats recalled the problems Al Smith faced in 1928, but it was a different country now, with Catholic American voting blocs having gained economic and political power in the prior decades and relative social acceptance. While a part of the electorate opted against Kennedy on religious grounds, it was fewer than would have 30 years earlier.

Kennedy struggled with Republicans and conservative Democrats over domestic issues, especially taxes and the economy. Both elements would prevent Kennedy's modest attempts at expanding New Deal programs. In foreign policy, his setbacks, such as the failed U.S.-supported attack on Cuba's Communist government during the Bay of Pigs invasion in 1961, were balanced out by Kennedy and his advisers successfully facing down the Soviet Union and negotiating with its leaders to remove nuclear weapons from Cuba during the Cuban Missile Crisis in 1962.

Some consider Kennedy's greatest achievement to be inspirational rather than legislative. Famous for his inaugural call to arms that advised people to ask what they could do for their country instead of what their country could do for them, Kennedy inspired young people to join his newly formed Peace Corps to assist people in need in developing countries and declared America's intentions to reach the moon by 1970. On civil rights, he was less hesitant than others, and he and his brother and attorney general, Robert Kennedy, made a show of supporting activists.

When Kennedy was assassinated in November 1963, the vice president, Lyndon B. Johnson, was sworn in as president. Johnson was a shrewd and savvy operator with years of Senate and House experience and had mainly been a conservative. The decisions Johnson and his fellow Democrats made in the tumultuous social climate of the 1960s, with the civil rights movement giving way to the Vietnam War conflict, would once again realign American politics for an entirely new era.

Chapter Six

POLITICAL PARTIES THEN AND NOW

Lyndon B. Johnson leveraged the massive goodwill Kennedy had built before his death to push through the Civil Rights Act of 1964. This legislation aimed to ban discrimination based on race, color, national origin, religion, age, or disability. Johnson's changes would encompass not only civil rights legislation, but also many liberal New Deal expansions that were the biggest since Roosevelt's. These measures, launched between 1964 and 1965, were collectively known as the Great Society programs. With new funding and new government agencies, Johnson and the liberal wing of the Democrats hoped to help the poor, fund schools, end discrimination in housing and immigration law, build housing, and otherwise wage a war on poverty.

The voting blocs and interest groups of the New Deal Coalition began to shift, too. Some opposed civil rights legislation, and the Democrats steadily lost southern white voters. Black voters had switched from Republican to Democrat during Roosevelt's tenure, the same party as many conservative southern white voters.

Many youth at the time distrusted the establishment and sought radical change. The Vietnam War, which began with limited troop deployments, expanded greatly under Johnson's presidency. This alienated liberal Democrats, especially students, and divided the party's establishment and more radical, leftist factions. Other groups were inspired by civil rights activism and grew tired of waiting for change. These included antiwar activists and students, women newly empowered as feminists, Latinx Americans, Native Americans, members of the LGBT+ community, and members of other identity-based movements who had been discriminated against and marginalized. Other radical groups, such as Students for a Democratic Society and the Black Panther party, along with Marxist, Communist, and Socialist groups, would form the Far Left faction called the New Left. These groups would push agendas leftward, even when they abstained or boycotted Democratic Party politics.

A New Realignment

Johnson's challenger in 1964 was Republican Barry Goldwater, Arizona's conservative senator. Goldwater firmly opposed the New Deal and its expansion, and he favored limited government on economic and social issues. His adherence to many conservative principles led many, especially Democrats, to call him extremist. Conservatives flocked to Goldwater, however. More than 1 million small donors, with 400,000 contributing less than $10 apiece, would support his campaign. Johnson beat Goldwater in 1964 with the highest share of the popular vote of anyone since James Monroe won uncontested in 1820. The *New York Times* declared, "Barry Goldwater not only lost the presidential election yesterday but the conservative cause as well."[13] Despite his loss, Goldwater's policy positions on taxes, small government, antagonism toward the welfare state, and a strong national defense would become the dominant and mainstream Republican policies of the coming decades.

The Democrats Implode

Meanwhile, the slow pace of reforms, continued and widespread racism, and police brutality resulted in expressions of rage from black communities nationwide. Riots flared up in hundreds of cities throughout the 1960s. Some of the worst occurred the year Martin Luther King Jr. was assassinated in April 1968. Johnson's failure to end the Vietnam War by 1968 was proving a political liability as well. Although accounts differ on his personal reasons for it, Johnson declared he would not seek reelection.

Robert Kennedy ran but was assassinated while on the campaign trail in California in June 1968. The Democrats soon split between the antiwar wing of the party, led by Senator Eugene McCarthy of Minnesota, and the establishment wing, represented by Hubert Humphrey. By this time, the antiwar movement had brought out hundreds of thousands to protest America's involvement in Vietnam for three years running. At the Democratic National Convention in Chicago, antiwar activists protested outside and in the streets, and their brutal repression by police was watched by shocked television audiences worldwide. Humphrey complained he could smell the tear gas in his shower at his hotel.

Within the convention hall, chaos ruled the proceedings. Some states had two different delegations competing to be recognized as their states' proper representatives. Until 1968, according to a report on National Public Radio,

The bitter battles among delegates at the 1968 Democratic National Convention in Chicago over whether to end the Vietnam War were instrumental in the party's defeat in that year's presidential race.

"powerful people and party bosses around the country picked delegates to the conventions ... There were factional battles at party conventions, but civilians were not involved until the general election."[14] The unruly convention, and the violence outside, projected to voters that Democrats could hardly contain disorder in their own party, much less be trusted with a nation many felt to be already imploding.

The Southern Strategy

Richard Nixon ran for president again in 1968. He ran partly on a law and order platform, believing that many Americans were tired and frightened from seeing constant rioting in their cities and on the news. Humphrey and others noted that this was directed mostly at conservative white voters. Known now as the southern strategy, Nixon hoped to peel off white conservative voters in great numbers from the South's dominant party, the Democrats, by appealing to white racism.

Nixon also opposed mandatory desegregation and promised to nominate conservative judges to the federal bench who would not aggressively press social change. He said civil rights could be achieved by volunteerism, charity, and economic opportunities provided via traditional conservative policies, such as tax breaks. These policies pushed the Republican party more rightward and alienated potential minority voters.

The wild card in 1968 turned out to be Alabama's segregationist governor, George Wallace, who ran for the Far Right American Independent Party and supported segregationist policies. Wallace's was one of the most successful third-party runs of the modern era, peeling votes from Republicans. Regardless, it was an extremely close election, and Nixon won by less than 100,000 votes.

The Nixon Era

In 1969, Nixon would declare a slow but steady withdrawal of U.S. forces from Vietnam to begin that year. In reality, the last U.S. troops did not withdraw from Vietnam until 1973. Still, the promise of lessened involvement in Vietnam and Nixon's foreign policy success in establishing diplomatic relations with a longtime enemy, China, poised him well for reelection in 1972. Democrats hoped to mobilize support for South Dakota's Senator George McGovern, a classic liberal in the New Deal mold.

McGovern waged a Populist and grassroots campaign that embraced left-wing policy positions. He brought in thousands of activists and volunteers, veterans of the 1960s movements. Controversially, McGovern and his allies instituted complex convention rules. The rules required female and minority representation, and downplayed the traditional convention power players, such as state party operatives, members of political machines, and organized labor. The convention itself became chaotic, running from early morning to late at night. McGovern's acceptance speech for the nomination was broadcast at 3:00 a.m., and most Americans never saw it.

The official platform was among the most left-leaning and liberal ever produced by an American political party. It included planks such as guaranteed employment for all citizens, aggressive actions on civil rights for women and LGBT+ people, and immediate withdrawal from Southeast Asia. Democratic voters had remained extremely divided on the ongoing Vietnam War. Meanwhile, many voters, the media, and others all considered the platform too radical.

Only eight years earlier, the Goldwater defeat had convinced some that the Republican Party would never recover and perhaps might even wither away, like the Whigs had. Now, Nixon

New rules at the Democratic Convention of 1972 inspired New York congresswoman Shirley Chisholm to become the first black candidate and the first woman to seek the presidential nomination for the Democrats.

defeated McGovern in one of the biggest electoral landslides ever with 520 votes to 17 votes. Democrats in Congress would hold on to their lead in the Senate and House.

Carter, Reagan, and the Birth of Modern Politics

From 1968 through the 1990s, the Democrats would only win a single presidential election. They would control the House and Senate, however, for some time. As Ryan Cooper wrote in the *Nation*, McGovern's

> *crushing defeat became the catalyst for a whole generation of Democratic politicians who rejected both the basic elements of New Deal liberalism and the dovish [peaceful] foreign policy of the New Left. From the 1970s through the Obama years, the Democrats would make their peace with many elements of the conservative economic and social agenda.*[15]

Before McGovern's defeat in 1972, Republican Party operatives burglarizing the Democratic National Committee headquarters at the Watergate apartment complex in Washington, D.C., had been caught. The investigation of this crime revealed Nixon's far-reaching paranoia and corruption and became known as the Watergate scandal. Before he could be impeached and removed from office, Nixon became the only U.S. president to resign from office in 1974. Vice President Gerald R. Ford was sworn in as president. Exhaustion and alienation seemed to set in, prompted by everything from several oil crises to a slow but ongoing decline in American manufacturing jobs, which would be sent overseas increasingly from the 1970s onwards.

Ford himself, in his inaugural speech, described the end of "our long national nightmare,"[16] but economic depression and stagnation were major problems during Ford's tenure. Many of these problems were beyond his control, but a general sense grew that Ford was incompetent.

The Democratic Party was eager to reclaim the presidency and in 1976, picked Jimmy Carter, a peanut farmer and Georgia senator, to run against Ford. Carter and running mate Walter Mondale were classic liberals. Carter took advantage of the national mood and campaigned as a Washington outsider, emphasizing his Christian background. As a seemingly wholesome newcomer promising a change, Carter narrowly defeated Ford and became the first president elected from the Deep South since Taylor in 1848.

An Era of Change

The 1970s into the 1980s would mark increasing polarization between the two parties. It was increasingly difficult for the Democrats to field liberal candidates for the presidency. Some members wanted to downplay liberal and left-wing stances in favor of centrist

Political Conventions: Then and Now

Early political conventions were very different from today's conventions. Before 1972, delegates to party nominating conventions were picked by powerful organizations that ran state parties. Extensive, often secret, backroom negotiations determined which candidates were nominated to run for president. Delegations from all the states would often vote on their favored candidates during the conventions, only making final decisions at this stage in the process. At the conventions, it would sometimes take multiple votes to determine the winning candidates.

After the chaotic Democratic National Convention in 1968, a commission headed by Senator George McGovern created new rules to follow. Direct primaries in the states, where voters picked candidates on primary day, were recommended. Both Democrats and Republicans adopted this model over the coming decades. Today, most states have direct primary elections. Primary winners are awarded delegates (often party officials and activists), who then pledge to support the candidates who won each state contest at their convention. In some primaries, a winner-takes-all approach means that a candidate earns all the delegates if they win a state. In proportional contests, if one candidate wins 60 percent of the vote, they are awarded about 60 percent of the delegates, while the remaining candidates are awarded the rest.

Today, most nominations are decided weeks in advance of the summer conventions during election years, leaving conventions to serve more as a marketing event that demonstrates party unity and promotes the party and its winning ticket for a national audience.

The days of heated negotiations to select candidates at national conventions are largely over. Instead, modern conventions are largely branding exercises that push the message of already selected candidates and party platforms.

and even right-wing policies. Simultaneously, several movements would fuel a Republican comeback.

From the 1970s on, conservative evangelical Christian voters were energized to overturn the 1973 Supreme Court Decision *Roe v. Wade*, which provided constitutional protections for access to abortion services. They also lent their votes to family values or traditional values issues, including opposition to certain aspects of the LGBT+ rights movement and feminism, as well as efforts to promote school prayer, anti-Communism, and other causes.

The religious right, as it came to be known, became a powerful voting bloc for a newer and more conservative Republican Party in the 1980s and 1990s. Televangelist preachers such as Pat Robertson and Jerry Falwell, founder of the Moral Majority organization, became powerful Republican operatives and leaders. Such organizations, including networks of churches, set up telephone hotlines, orchestrated large direct mail and phone campaigns, and knocked on doors to get out the vote. They also marched and ran for local and state offices and eventually voted their own candidates into the Senate and House.

The two parties began to represent two different cultures, rather than simply different groups of voters. Voters were drawn by Republican promises of lower taxes and pro-business policies, law and order, tough-on-crime policies, and a commitment to the Second Amendment and gun rights. The gun lobby, via the National Rifle Association (NRA) and related organizations, has been firmly identified with the GOP since the 1970s.

Marketing the Parties

From the Kennedy era onward, modern political campaigns have been increasingly waged via television and other visual media. Marketing candidates and parties became as important as promoting their platforms. With the nation seemingly divided down the middle between conservatives and liberals, political operatives for hire—such as consultants, pollsters, and public relations professionals—came to dominate elite political circles.

Image and perception played a big role in Jimmy Carter's presidency. The economic situation in the United States remained poor during his term. The longer the oil crisis and recession went, the more it was used as a sign of Carter's weakness. When Iranians took 52 American diplomats and citizens hostage at the U.S. Embassy in Tehran, the 444-day standoff, in which Carter failed to win the hostages their freedom, further damaged him.

Republicans took their chance to reclaim the White House in 1980. California's conservative former governor Ronald Reagan promised voters a return to patriotism, law and order, and economic prosperity. Long before President Donald Trump adopted the phrase

Ronald Reagan's (right) success in pushing out Jimmy Carter (left) in the 1980 election is considered by some to be a realigning election.

during the 2016 campaign cycle, one of Reagan's slogans was "Let's Make America Great Again." The cowboy confidence of the Hollywood actor and a desire to leave the misery of the 1970s behind made many so-called Reagan Democrats cross party lines. Reagan also attacked the high crime in the cities as signs of weaknesses leftover from the New Deal and Great Society efforts and hoped to downsize these long-standing programs. Reagan's landslide over

Carter also helped his party win control of the Senate for the first time since the mid–1950s.

Reagan's policies were hostile toward unions, taxation, and government bureaucracy, especially what Republicans referred to as the welfare state, which included poverty assistance programs. The plan to lower taxes and hope that American corporations and business owners would then hire more workers and

Money in Politics

One criticism of the current electoral system is the role of money in politics. Modern voters are constantly exposed to political content via cable television on Fox News, MSNBC, and other channels and online via social media platforms and countless websites. Tremendous amounts of cash from interest groups, corporations, lobbyists, and others have become standard. Like an arms race in which each enemy tries to arm itself with more weapons, Republicans and Democrats need to raise more money every year or risk being outspent by the other party. The reliance on huge amounts of money, even for minor congressional races, good-government advocates say, leads to a form of legal corruption in politics. Politicians are more likely to favor the interests of large corporate campaign donors than the concerns of regular citizens.

jump-start the economy was called supply-side or trickle-down economics. The GOP claimed that benefits would trickle down to working people at all levels. Democrats attacked this idea.

Reagan's economic policies, including large cuts to aid for the poor, would cause a mini-depression early in his term, but a recovery in 1983 led to an economic boom. The hidden costs were enormous budget deficits and growing poverty. The traditional liberals on the Democratic side had a hard time challenging Reagan when the economy recovered. The spirit of the times seemed to reward excess and self-interest, and Reagan again represented that confidence as embodied in the famous campaign ad that stated, "It's Morning in America."

Liberalism Loses Steam

While still hanging onto the House, Democrats had poor luck with liberal presidential tickets in the 1980s. Reagan's 1984 landslide reelection over Minnesota Senator Walter Mondale, Carter's vice president, was as predictable as it was overwhelming. Mondale's efforts at being honest, largely by promising to raise taxes to fix the deficit, were ineffective—few wanted higher taxes. Voters flocked to Reagan's foreign policy and anti-Communism stance. White voters, including women, overwhelmingly supported Reagan, as well as about a quarter of Democrats and nearly half of moderates.

In 1988, Reagan's vice president, George H. W. Bush, ran against Democratic Massachusetts governor Michael Dukakis, an outspoken liberal. The presidential race was a referendum on the Reagan years. Dukakis was challenged from the Left by longtime civil rights leader Jesse Jackson and his National Rainbow Coalition, which called for a union of voters across lines of ethnicity, religion, ability, and gender to demand protection for social programs and self-empowerment for marginalized people.

After locking up the nomination, Dukakis could not convince Americans to change course. The repeated use of "liberal" as a bad word and airing of negative campaign ads further hurt the Democrat, and Bush won easily. With two major presidential defeats, party loyalists and media questioned whether America itself had not turned rightward generally, which would explain why firmly liberal candidates were having trouble. The idea, however, ignored many other factors in Mondale and Dukakis's losses, including Reagan's popularity, the candidates' weaknesses, and the economic fortunes that no one could seem to control.

Rebranding Democrats: The Clinton Years

Leading into the 1992 election cycle, some Democrats thought the party should tack to the center. Among these were the New Democrats led by the youthful, charismatic Democratic governor of Arkansas, William "Bill" Jefferson Clinton. Democratic leadership put its faith in both Clinton's personal appeal and in his embrace of more center and even right-leaning positions, including pro-business leanings. Clinton challenged the incumbent Bush in the 1992 election. During the campaign, Bush came across as out of touch with Americans, while the Democrats masterfully used television to position Clinton as in touch and sympathetic to Americans suffering through a recession. A major third-party challenge by the self-financed billionaire Ross Perot took away votes from Bush due to Perot's conservatism, and Clinton won 43 percent of the popular vote, versus Bush's 37.4 percent and Perot's impressive 18.9 percent.

The Clinton campaign unfolded in a new media landscape. In the cable news era, 24-hour coverage of politics and other events would become another battleground in the war of ideas and brands for both parties. Clinton and others now also relied heavily on polls. If public opinion shifted one way or the other on a topic that split Americans nearly equally, Clinton and other centrists were likely to bend with the shifting wind.

Another successful Clinton strategy was triangulation. This meant taking classical Republican or conservative positions and adopting them outright or even partially. In doing so, Republicans could not attack Clinton or other Democrats on these issues, and they would then gain an edge in voters interested in that issue. New Democrats saw overly liberal platforms as outdated and unpopular. Clinton declared in his 1996

State of the Union address that "the era of big Government is over."[17] He pushed for tougher sentencing for criminals in response to a perceived crime wave and also signed Republican-supported legislation to defund welfare programs. He even signed legislation in 1996 to "end welfare as we know it."[18]

The New Democrats believed that Americans had grown more conservative. Pollsters and strategists flocked to tell candidates how to win obscure demographics. An obsession grew to capture swing voters, those who might support a candidate from either party, given the right motivations. One famous example was the supposed "soccer moms," who represented middle-class suburban working mothers. Consultants believed they were a key constituency that would help Clinton win reelection in 1996 over Kansas Senate Republican Bob Dole, with little real evidence this would make a difference. Clinton did win the 1996 election, capturing 379 electoral votes, while Dole

Political consultants, such as James Carville (center), have become nearly as important to party politics in recent decades as the candidates themselves. These consultants often become famous and have long careers in politics and the media.

The Republican Revolution: "The Contract with America"

One of the most important realignments in modern politics occurred not during a hotly contested presidential race, but during the 1994 midterm elections, halfway through Clinton's first term. Democrats had controlled the House of Representatives for decades.

At the time, the Republican congressman from Georgia and House Minority Whip—the traditional leadership position of the congressional minority party who "whips" their party's congressional colleagues into line to vote for policies—was Newt Gingrich. Gingrich led the effort to draft a list of promises to voters that Republicans pledged to keep if they took control of the House. Among these were plans to shrink the government, lower taxes, reform public welfare programs, and more.

Called "The Contract with America," it was unusual and pioneering in the way it offered concrete legislation that would be voted on. Though many of the measures would later stall in Congress, it was released six weeks before Election Day and is credited with helping the GOP gain fifty-four seats in the House and nine in the Senate, thus taking congressional control entirely from their Democratic rivals.

Political observers often credit this stunning upset with forcing President Clinton and other Democrats to compromise more with conservative positions in the coming years.

received 159 votes.

There was much bad blood over the very close 2000 election. Democrat Al Gore, Clinton's vice president, won the popular vote. However, the election was decided by a Supreme Court decision on whether to recount a very controversial vote in the state of Florida. George W. Bush, former governor of Texas and son of the previous president George H. W. Bush, was declared the winner. It seemed that the two campaigns did not differ to great extremes over ideology. Bush insisted he was not like the harsh conservatives of old, but rather a conservative who was compassionate and would be moderate on most social issues. Gore attempted to run on the economic boom of the Clinton years, Progressive social issues, and centrist to conservative economic ones. Meanwhile, Gore tried to distance himself from the scandal and impeachment Clinton had suffered in 1998.

The Bush versus Gore campaign highlighted another troubling aspect of modern politics, and that was the speed at which scandals and small missteps—often called gaffes—dominated the coverage that many Americans watched and that helped decide their votes. It was a shift from actual issues that affected most citizens to horse race journalism. The media was often more interested in how candidates were judged, their personalities, and polling data.

THE JOURNEY AHEAD

The 2000s seemingly solidified the two major parties into two sides that not only disagree on crucial issues, but also represent different cultures entirely. Mostly, the Republican Party has represented conservative voters, while the Democrats are identified with liberal and Progressive causes. Still, the policies and constituencies of the respective parties have continued to shift.

The Culture Wars

Whereas Democrats, and especially liberals, were once considered nonaggressive on foreign policy, current Republicans and Democrats largely conduct similar policies, including foreign interventions. Both parties are also pro-business, while the Democrats still try to curb the worst impulses of businesses with regulations.

Voters today seem to vote according to their positions on the so-called "culture wars." For example,

many Republicans still vote in support of their constitutional right to own firearms, restricting access to abortion services, and other typically conservative causes.

The election of Democratic Illinois Senator Barack Obama to the presidency in 2008 was seen as a breath of fresh air by many, however, it also underscored the resistance that many Americans had to social change, including enfranchisement of African Americans. Democratic efforts to introduce the health insurance program commonly known as the Affordable Care Act, or Obamacare, were met with heavy resistance by conservatives. These resistance efforts, led by some grassroots movements and funded by groups such as Americans for Prosperity, grew into the Tea Party movement. While not a traditional political party, it was made up of many groups opposing various Democratic positions, especially the quest for

Opposition to many policies of the new Obama administration came from Tea Party protesters and activists, who were an even more conservative wing of the Republican Party.

universal health care.

Republicans fought almost all new legislation and actions by Obama during his two terms. In addition, they continue to oppose many of the social justice efforts of Democrats and liberal and leftist activists. These included the push to legalize marriage for LGBT+ Americans; efforts at curbing racism and police brutality, pioneered by activists such as the members of the Black Lives Matter movement; immigration reform;

environmental activism and efforts to curb climate change; gun control efforts; and much more.

Insurgent Campaigns

By the 2016 election cycle, many voters were exhausted by several presidential terms of war, political infighting, and business as usual. Both Republicans and Democrats were criticized for content-free campaigns. It seemed that politicians very rarely said what they meant, if they were saying anything at all. Two insurgent political campaigns, one on each side of the political divide, would upend politics as usual, at least initially.

During the 2016 election cycle, American voters witnessed the transformation of television reality show host and real-estate developer Donald Trump into a viable presidential candidate. Trump, formerly a political moderate, rose to fame as part of the birther movement, which challenged President Obama's citizenship (claiming he was born overseas) during his term.

Trump spoke out against Mexicans, immigrants, Muslims, and other groups. His aggressive performances in television debates thrilled a growing number of conservatives. Trump's Populist campaign used anti-Obama resentment, the Twitter social media platform, and the general unhappiness with the political and economic direction of the country to masterful effect. He shocked many when he won the Republican nomination and challenged Democrat Hillary Clinton, the former first lady, senator, and secretary of

Some people consider 2016 a realigning election since the unexpected victory of Donald Trump showed that an outsider could clean house against establishment Republicans. Despite this, Trump adopted more or less traditional Republican policies once elected.

Primaries: Open and Closed

Different types of primaries in presidential party politics are held in various states. The main categories are open and closed. Fourteen states have closed primaries, while the rest have open primaries, or they utilize the political caucus to select nominating convention delegates.

In an open primary, voters affiliated with any party, or no party at all, may vote in the primary of any party that is on the ballot. Rules restrict voters from voting in multiple primaries during an election season. Some people criticize such primaries because members of other parties can manipulate primary contests to favor their party in a general election.

In closed primaries, only registered Democrats, for example, may vote in a Democratic primary. Rules vary by state, but some states allow someone to pick a party affiliation on the day of voting, while others require picking the party earlier on.

A handful of states and territories of the United States use a caucus system, where groups of people gather and choose openly which candidates to support. In Iowa, for example, voters assemble on election day in the state's 1,681 voting precincts, and each delivers proportional delegates to competing candidates.

state, for the presidency. Trump appealed to many Americans, who had seen their communities destroyed by jobs being sent overseas or were otherwise struggling in the current economy, by promising to "Make America Great Again."

Senator Bernie Sanders of Vermont, an Independent who generally voted with Democrats, challenged Clinton in the Democratic primaries. Mainstream Democrats were surprised when Sanders's campaign generated great excitement. With unapologetically left-wing positions, including promises of free health care for all, free college education, and college debt forgiveness, Sanders opened up debate on issues that New Democrats, including Clinton, had long ago deemed settled. Clinton eventually clinched the nomination, defeating Sanders's insurgent, social democratic campaign within the Democratic Party, but liberal and Progressive issues were back on the table for a new generation.

Many centrist and center-left Democrats blamed Sanders for damaging Clinton in the primary campaign. They felt that her loss to Donald Trump in the presidential election was due in part to Sanders, although he campaigned for Clinton and endorsed her in the general election. Others accused Green Party candidate Jill

In 2016, internal divisions within the Democratic Party existed between the establishment centrist wing represented by Hillary Clinton and the more leftist Progressive wing that Senator Bernie Sanders represented during the primary season against Clinton.

Stein of taking votes away from Clinton in very close races in formerly safe Democratic strongholds, such as Wisconsin, Michigan, and Pennsylvania. The Clinton campaign was also accused of failing to mount an effective organizing ground game in those states. Many also credited Trump's victory to campaign promises of jobs and reinvestment, while criticizing Clinton for not offering clear objectives and policies to believe in.

Left-wing critics have consistently criticized New Democrats like Clinton for a rightward shift in the Democratic Party. For example, Sanders attacked free-trade policies and measures such as the North American Free Trade Agreement (NAFTA), passed in 1993 by Bill Clinton, as anti-worker. They want the Democrats to concentrate on bread-and-butter economic leftism and reenergize the party with New Deal-like policies, such as some

Bipartisanship in an Age of Confrontation

While divides over many issues continue to dominate modern politics, recent examples of Democrats and Republicans working together on legislative measures and goals give hope to those who value consensus and cooperation.

For example, in 2015, Senator Lamar Alexander, a Tennessee Republican, worked with Senator Patty Murray, a Washington Democrat, on an education policy overhaul bill called the Every Student Succeeds Act. Both sides agreed to transfer certain powers regarding schools and teacher evaluations from the federal government to the states.

Meanwhile, in 2011, several House Republicans, including Virginia's Eric Cantor, partnered with House Democrats, including Jim McDermott of Washington, Michigan's Sander Levin, and California's Sam Farr, to sponsor deals favoring free trade with South Korea, Panama, and Colombia.

Republicans and Democrats have also aligned on foreign policy matters. A majority of both parties collaborated on measures to support America's primary ally in the Middle East, the state of Israel. Meanwhile, many of the same have agreed on economic sanctions against nations, including Syria, Iran, and Russia, as the United States became more interested in the Syrian Civil War, which began in 2011, and the refugee crisis it has created.

of Sanders's proposals. Some even began to wonder, such as Democrats had in the 1930s, whether hyper-aggressive capitalism itself was to blame. They attacked the corporatism of both Democrats and Republicans.

Moving Forward

The Tea Party movement and the Sanders campaign demonstrated how both right- and left-wing forces in America's two major parties have begun to push back against more safely centrist philosophies. As of 2018, Trump has fulfilled a few of his promises to working-class voters, but some believe many of his policies have actually harmed them. His administration's efforts to dismantle government regulations and enforcement, aggressive immigration enforcement, and attempts to ban immigrants and visitors from several Muslim-majority nations have angered Democrats and Progressives, inspiring protests and legislative battles. Still, Trump's base has firmly supported him and is thought likely to continue to do so. Establishment Republicans seem to have few real policy differences with Trump, even though news reports before and during the 2016 election predicted the possible collapse of the Republican Party.

The Democrats are hoping they can regroup for upcoming elections. A pro-Sanders faction continues to support bolder policies that would have been considered extreme by 1990s-era Democrats. They hope to change the landscape and make it possible to institute social democratic reforms, with nations such as Norway and Sweden as the model. Centrist Democrats continue to fight these Progressive policies and accuse this faction of abandoning identity politics and of desiring unrealistic change that will alienate an America they feel is more conservative.

The future of political parties in the United States has never been predictable. Will leftists upset with centrist Democrats leave and form a third party, or will they continue to attempt to reform the Democrats in their image, despite fierce resistance? Will future voters be alienated by Trump and others on right-wing policies, and will this generate a backlash, such as a left-leaning one to match the Tea Party backlash against Obama? The story of political parties in America continues to unfold in real time.

Notes

Introduction:
The Dawn of American Politics

1. "The Constitution of the United States: A Transcription," National Archives, accessed on February 2, 2018. www.archives.gov/founding-docs/constitution-transcript.
2. "From Thomas Jefferson to George Washington, 23 May 1792," Founders Online, accessed on February 2, 2018. founders.archives.gov/documents/Jefferson/01-23-02-0491.
3. Quoted in Gordon S. Wood, *Revolutionary Characters: What Made the Founders Different*. New York, NY: Penguin Press, 2006, p. 153.

Chapter Two:
Democrats and Whigs

4. David Edwin Harrell, Jr., Edwin S. Gaustad, John B. Boles, Sally Foreman Griffith, Randall M. Miller, Randall B. Woods, *Unto a Good Land: A History of the American People*. Grand Rapids, MI: Wm. B. Eerdmans Publishing Company, 2005, p. 377.

Chapter Three:
Republicans and Democrats

5. P. R. Fendall, et al., *The Northern Man with Southern Principles and the Southern Man with American Principles*. Washington, D.C.: Peter Force, 1840.

Chapter Four:
The New Century

6. Quoted in "Today in History—March 19: William Jennings Bryan," Library of Congress, accessed on January 30, 2018. www.loc.gov/item/today-in-history/march-19.
7. William Roscoe Thayer, *Theodore Roosevelt*. New York, NY: Grosset & Dunlap, 1919. www.gutenberg.org/ebooks/2386.
8. The New York Times Staff, "Unusual Political Career of Calvin Coolidge, Never Defeated for an Office." *New York Times*, January 6, 1933. www.nytimes.com/learning/general/onthisday/bday/0704.html.
9. "'A Chicken in Every Pot' Political Ad and Rebuttal Article in New York Times," National Archives, accessed on January 28, 2017. catalog.archives.gov/id/187095.

Chapter Five:
The New Deal Era

10. Tim Jones, "Dewey Defeats Truman," *Chicago Tribune*, accessed on January 30, 2018. www.chicagotribune.com/news/nationworld/politics/chi-chicagodays-deweydefeats-story-story.html.

11. Charles Van Doren and Robert McHenry, *Webster's Guide to American History: A Chronological, Geographical, and Biographical Survey and Compendium.* Springfield, MA: G. & C. Merriam Company, 1971, p. 533.

12. David A. Graham, "If You Give Me a Week, I Might Think of One," *The Atlantic*, May 27, 2016. www.theatlantic.com/notes/2016/05/if-you-give-me-a-week-i-might-think-of-one/484556.

Chapter Six:
Political Parties Then and Now

13. Lee Edwards, "Barry M. Goldwater: The Most Consequential Loser in American Politics," Heritage Foundation, July 3, 2014. www.heritage.org/political-process/report/barry-m-goldwater-the-most-consequential-loser-american-politics#_ftn1.

14. Linda Wertheimer, "1968 Convention Sparked Reforms for Democrats," National Public Radio, August 28, 2008. www.npr.org/templates/story/story.php?storyId=93937947.

15. Ryan Cooper, "The Last Populist: George McGovern's Alternative Path for the Democratic Party," *The Nation*, August 8, 2017. www.thenation.com/article/the-last-populist.

16. Quoted in "Special Display at the National Archives Remembers President Ford," National Archives, December 27, 2006. www.archives.gov/press/press-releases/2007/nr07-36.html.

17. William J. Clinton, "Address Before a Joint Session of the Congress on the State of the Union, January 23, 1996," The American Presidency Project, accessed on January 30, 2018. www.presidency.ucsb.edu/ws/?pid=53091.

18. "Text of President Clinton's Announcement on Welfare Legislation," *New York Times*, August 1, 1996. www.nytimes.com/1996/08/01/us/text-of-president-clinton-s-announcement-on-welfare-legislation.html.

For More Information

Books

Bjornlund, Lydia, and Richard Bell. *Modern Political Parties*. Minneapolis, MN: Core Library/ABDO Publishing, 2017. This book introduces readers to the two-party system of the United States and details their origins and roles in contemporary politics.

Carey, Charles W. *African-American Political Leaders*. New York, NY: Facts on File, 2011. This book has biographies and photos of African American politicians at the local and federal levels.

Cunningham, Anne C. *Women Political Leaders*. New York, NY: Enslow Publishing, 2017. This volume collects stories of famous female political leaders, from women of ancient civilizations to modern political players.

Lansford, Tom. *Political Participation and Voting Rights*. Broomall, PA: Mason Crest, 2017. The focus of this book is how voting works as a form of political participation. Lansford also provides a mandate for the actions and policies of those who participate in politics.

McPherson, Stephanie Sammartino. *Political Parties: From Nominations to Victory Celebrations*. Minneapolis, MN: Lerner Publications, 2016. This book zeroes in on the inner workings of political parties and the steps they take to nominate and elect party members to government posts.

Websites

Democrats

www.democrats.org
This website is the official website of the Democratic Party of the United States. It has information on the party's platform, history, leaders, organization, and more.

GOP

www.gop.com
The official website of the Republican National Committee has information on the platform as well as history and issues.

The Library of Congress

www.loc.gov
The United States Library of Congress has one of the largest digital archives of primary source documents relating to the history of the United States, including many political cartoons.

United States House of Representatives

www.house.gov
This is the official website of the House of Representatives of the United States. The website has information on current representatives, legislative activity, and what the House of Representatives is.

United States Senate

www.senate.gov
The official website of the United States Senate has information on senators, committees, and legislation.

Index

A
abolitionists, 29, 35, 39, 41
Adams, John, 6, 19–21, 25
Adams, John Quincy, 25, 27, 29
Alabama, 40, 77
Alien and Sedition Acts, 20
American Civil War, 6, 37, 42, 45, 48–49
American Party, 39
American Railway Union (ARU), 67
American Revolution, 11, 17–18, 25
American System, 29
anti-Federalists, 13, 15, 21
Arizona, 33, 75
assassination, 44, 55, 73, 75

B
balance of powers, 6, 18
Ballinger, Richard, 56
Baltimore, Maryland, 27, 40
Banking Act of 1933, 64
Bank of England, 16
Bank of the United States, 16, 27, 29
Bank War, 29
Battle of New Orleans, 25
Bay of Pigs invasion, 73
Bell, John, 42
Biddle, Nicholas, 29
black codes, 44–45
Black Lives Matter, 89
Black Panther party, 75
Bonus Army, 64
Booth, John Wilkes, 44
Breckinridge, John C., 40, 42
broadsides, 11
Brooks, Preston, 41
Brown v. Board of Education, 71
Bryan, William Jennings, 7, 51–53, 56–57

Buchanan, James, 39–40, 42
Bull Moose Party, 56–57
Bureau of Corporations, 55
Burr, Aaron, 19–21
Bush, George H. W., 83–84, 86–87
Bush, George W., 7, 86–87
Butler, Andrew, 41

C
Calhoun, John C., 29, 33
California, 33–34, 75, 87, 93
Carnegie, Andrew, 49
Carter, Jimmy, 7, 79, 81–83
Cass, Lewis, 33
Catholic, 29, 37–38, 59, 61, 68, 72
Charleston, South Carolina, 39
Chicago Democratic Convention, 51
Clay, Henry, 25, 27, 29, 30–33, 37
Cleveland, Grover, 51, 53, 69
Clinton, Bill, 7, 84–87, 92
Clinton, Hillary, 7, 90–92
Cold War, 68–69
Compromise of 1850, 33, 35
Confederacy, 42, 44, 48
conflict, 9, 17, 20, 23, 39–40, 42, 45, 49, 57, 73
Constitutional Convention, 11, 13
Constitutional Union Party, 42
Coolidge, Calvin, 59–61
Copperheads, 42
corrupt bargain, 25
Cox, James M., 59
Cuban Missile Crisis, 73

D
Davis, John W., 59
Debs, Eugene V., 57, 67

Democratic-Republicans, 6, 17, 19–22, 25–26, 32
Dewey, Thomas, 68–70
Douglas, Stephen A., 37, 40, 42
Dukakis, Michael, 84

E
Eisenhower, Dwight D., 69, 71–72
Era of Good Feelings, 22

F
Farmers' Alliances, 51
Federalists, 6, 9, 11, 13–15, 17–22, 25–26, 29
Federal Deposit Insurance Corporation (FDIC), 64
Federal Reserve Act, 57
Federal Trade Commission (FTC), 55
Fillmore, Millard, 34, 39
First Party System, 22, 25–26
Florida, 7, 86
Founding Fathers, 13, 19
Framers, 11
Free Silver Movement, 51, 53
Free-Soil Party, 33
Frémont, John C., 39

G
General Welfare Clause, 16–17
Gilded Age, 47–51
Gold Bug Democrats, 53
Goldwater, Barry, 75, 77
Gore, Al, 7, 86–87
Grand Old Party (GOP), 37, 81, 83, 86
Grant, Ulysses S., 45, 47–48
Great Depression, 7, 62–63, 68
Greeley, Horace, 37, 47
Green Party, 8, 91

H
Hamilton, Alexander, 13–14, 16–19, 21
Harding, Warren G., 59, 61

Harrison, Benjamin, 51
Harrison, William Henry, 30
Hayes, Rutherford B., 47
Henry, Patrick, 13
Homestead Acts, 39
Hoover, Herbert, 61–64
Hoovervilles, 63–64
Hughes, Charles E., 57
Humphrey, Hubert, 75–76

I
immigrants, 20, 37–38, 49, 68, 90, 93
Indian Wars, 30

J
Jackson, Andrew, 6, 23–25, 27, 29–30, 55
Jacksonian democracy, 6, 25, 27, 30
Jackson, Michigan, 37
Jay Treaty, 19
Jeffersonians, 18–19, 21, 26
Jefferson, Thomas, 6, 13–14, 16–22, 27
Jim Crow laws, 47–48
Johnson, Andrew, 44–45
Johnson, Lyndon B., 9, 73–75

K
Kansas, 37, 39–41, 66, 85
Kansas-Nebraska Act, 37
Kennedy, John F., 71–74
Kennedy, Robert, 73, 75, 81
Knights of Labor, 51
Know-Nothing movement, 37–39
Korean War, 69, 71
Ku Klux Klan (KKK), 47, 59–60

L
La Follette, Robert M., 60
laissez-faire, 59, 63
Landon, Alf, 66
Lecompton Constitution, 39
Lee, Robert E., 44
LGBT+ community, 74, 77, 87, 89

Libertarians, 8
Liberty Party, 33
Lincoln, Abraham, 6, 8, 42–44
Lodge, Henry Cabot, 59
"log cabin and hard cider" campaign, 30
lynching, 47

M
Madison, James, 16–18, 20–22
Magnum, Willie Person, 30
Manifest Destiny, 32
McClellan, George B., 44
McGovern, George, 77, 79, 80
McKinley, William, 7, 53, 55
Mellon, Andrew, 49
Military Reconstruction Acts, 45
Mondale, Walter, 79, 83–84

N
National Bank, 16–18, 30
National Democratic Party, 53
National Farmer's Alliance, 51
National Grange, 51
National Labor Relations Act, 66
National Labor Relations Board (NLRB),
    66
National Republicans, 27, 29
National Rifle Association (NRA), 81
Native Americans, 23, 25, 27, 29, 74
nativists, 38
Nebraska Territory, 37
Necessary and Proper Clause, 17
Nevada, 33
New Deal Coalition, 66, 69, 74
New Deal programs, 7, 65–66, 68, 71,
    73–75, 77, 79, 82, 92
New Mexico, 33
19th Amendment, 59
Nixon, Richard, 7, 71–72, 76–77, 79

O
Obama, Barack, 7, 79, 88–90, 94

P
Panic of 1893, 53
Parker, Alton B., 55
Payne-Aldrich Tariff Act, 56
Philadelphia, Pennsylvania, 38
Pierce, Franklin, 35–37
Pinchback, Pinckney Benton Stewart
    (P. B. S.), 45–46
Pinchot, Gifford, 56
Pittsburgh, Pennsylvania, 37
political machine, 26, 40, 48, 77
Polk, James K., 30, 32–33
popular sovereignty, 33
Populists, 51–52, 56, 67, 77, 90
Progressives, 7, 49, 52–53, 56–57, 59, 64,
    68–69, 86, 88, 91–94
Prohibition, 61
Protestants, 38

R
Rankin, Jeannette, 57
Reagan, Ronald, 7, 79, 81–84
recession, 30, 69, 81, 84
Reconstruction, 44–45, 47, 50
robber barons, 49
Rockefeller, John D., 49–50
Roe v. Wade, 81
Roosevelt, Franklin Delano, 7, 64–66,
    68, 71, 74
Roosevelt, Theodore, 53–57, 60

S
scandal, 20, 47, 56, 79, 86–87
Schuyler, Elizabeth, 17
Scott, Winfield, 35
Second Bank of the United States, 27, 29
Second Party System, 29
Securities and Exchange Commission
    (SEC), 66
segregation, 9, 71, 77
Seward, William H., 40
Seymour, Horatio, 45

sharecropping, 45

Sherman, William Tecumseh, 44

slavery, 6, 8, 19, 23, 25, 29–30, 32–35, 37, 39, 41–42, 44–45, 50

Socialists, 57, 61, 64, 66–67, 75

"southern strategy," 7, 76–77

Soviet Union, 68, 72–73

Spanish-American War, 53

Square Deal, 55

Stanton, Edwin, 45

States' Rights Democratic Party, 69

Stevenson, Adlai, 69, 71

Sumner, Charles, 41

Supreme Court, 7, 18, 20, 29, 57, 71, 81, 86

T

Taft, William Howard, 55–57

Taylor, Zachary, 33–34, 79

Tea Party, 88–89, 93–94

temperance, 29, 49, 61

Texas, 30, 32, 86

Third Party System, 50

Tilden, Samuel, 47

Truman, Harry, 68–70

Trump, Donald, 7, 81, 90–94

12th Amendment, 20

22nd Amendment, 71

Tyler, John, 30, 32

U

Union, 23, 33–35, 42, 44–45

Union Army, 45

United States Census, 23

urbanization, 49

U.S. Constitution, 6, 11, 14, 16–18

Utah, 33

V

Van Buren, Martin, 26, 30, 32–33

Vietnam War, 7, 73–77

Virginia, 17–18, 20, 42, 93

W

Warmoth, Henry Clay, 45

War of 1812, 22, 25, 30

Washington, Booker T., 55

Washington, D.C., 10, 18, 21, 44, 64, 79

Washington, George, 6, 13–19, 25

Watson, Tom, 56

Weaver, James B., 51

Webster, Daniel, 27, 30, 33, 37

Whig party, 6, 9, 29–31, 33, 35, 37–38, 48, 77

White House, 21, 30, 59, 81

White, Hugh L., 30

Willkie, Wendell, 68

Wilson, Woodrow, 57, 59

World War I, 57, 64, 67

World War II, 68, 69

X

XYZ Affair, 20

Picture Credits

About the Author

Philip Wolny is a writer and editor hailing from Queens, New York. He has written numerous titles on politics, culture, and American and world history. Some of his credits include *The New Nation* (Early American History), *Colonialism: A Primary Source Analysis* (Primary Sources of Political Systems), *The Underground Railroad: A Primary Source History of the Journey to Freedom* (Primary Sources in American History), *Gun Rights: Interpreting the Constitution* (Understanding the United States Constitution), *Holodomor: The Ukrainian Famine-Genocide* (Bearing Witness: Genocide and Ethnic Cleansing), and many more. Wolny earned a degree in English from the State University of New York at Stony Brook and a masters in Euroculture from Jagiellonian University in Krakow, Poland, and has worked in trade journalism and publishing for two decades. He continues to reside in New York with his wife, Amanda, and daughter, Lucy.